Crashing

by

William Trent Pancoast

Blazing Flowers Press

INTERNATIONAL STANDARD BOOK
NUMBER: 978-0692627235

for Deby

ALSO BY WILLIAM TRENT PANCOAST

Wildcat, a novel

Valley Real Estate, a novel

Vietnam. Fucking Vietnam, stories

Chapter One

In its brochure that is sent to prospective teachers, the Oakridge Board of Education boasts that every major faith is represented by the churches of Oakridge. The Methodists, Lutherans, and Episcopalians are mainstays while the Baptists now control the part of town on the east side of the Penn Central tracks. The Holy Rollers, whose membership is down to a dozen eccentric old men, are leaving town next month.

Among the thirty-three churches in Oakridge there are churches for the poor, others for the middle class, and a couple for rich folks. To be sure, this is an oversimplification. No church in Oakridge would bar any person from entering its sanctuary because of social standing.

There are more bars than churches in Oakridge, though this is a statistic that only a perverse or anti-social mind might discover or have use for. The state of Ohio controls the number of bars in town or there would doubtless be many more. The bars, like the churches, are frequented by stratified groups of society. Like the ministers, no self-respecting barkeep in Oakridge will refuse service to a customer because he is different from the regulars. Mostly though there is no need for either the ministers or barkeeps to concern themselves since people in Oakridge usually go where they have come to believe they belong.

The Oakridge Country Club, Oakridge's version of social apartheid, does not, unlike the churches and bars, allow just anyone past its stone gates. Doctors, lawyers, businessmen, and rich folks, no questions asked abut the origin of their wealth, populate the stately clubhouse, golf course, tennis courts, and pool. Later on this Saturday evening in August, there will be a pool party at the country club. At that party, the editor of the *Oakridge Chronicle* will announce the winners of the 1977 Who's Who in Oakridge Award.

The Grotto, a bar located uptown on Main Street, caters mostly to young working men—laborers and factory workers. The bar is long and dim, the floor originally linoleum but now eroded to a black asphalt-like composition. A long bar matches the room's length, and a go-go girl is gyrating on the small stage at one end of it, twirling around the pole, watching herself in the mirror, while patrons sit numbly after a week of meaningless labors, drinking their beers and watching her.

Saturday night in Oakridge is the night that provides an escape from the gritty, depressing weekday life in a factory town. Smoke from barbecues drifts through the neighborhoods. Folks sit under shade trees in backyards with their coolers of beer and pop. Children's voices echo through it all, even the little ones sensing that it is once again Saturday night and the rules will be relaxed, curfews lifted.

As the evening draws onward, the traffic flow increases, the local police begin their drunk driver vigilance, phones ring and plans are made, the bars fill, cars screech around corners as the Camaros, Firebirds, Dodge Hemis, and Mustangs warm up their motors and tires for the parade around the square.

Jean Holz sits in the library of her spacious brick home. She is a writer of literary fiction and has published several stories. The problem for twenty years has been that she has not had time to write. But this fall she is signed up for a creative writing course at the Cranston campus of Ohio State. She will have the time now to devote to writing a novel. Her son Mark is 20 and just finished his second year of college at Ohio State. Her husband John is slated to be the next vice president of Blatt Metal Works. No worries for her, she is thinking as she puts the beginning of a story in her desk and goes about getting ready to go the country club where she will meet John for dinner.

In the country club locker room, John Holz sits on the wooden bench savoring the air conditioning after the humid round of golf he just completed. Gets old playing with a bunch of hackers and he is glad the round is over. He thinks of getting his hands on a big gin and tonic and grabs his towel and heads for the showers.

Uptown at the Grotto, Mark Holz sits with Frank Baker along the wall. A year ago Mark would have had no reason to be in the Grotto, but he's a working man now. When he told his dad he wasn't working on his golf game anymore—John wanted him to continue to try and make the Ohio State team—he was told to get a job. So he did. All summer he has worked the shipping dock at the carton company with Frank, a guy a couple years ahead of him in high school and just out of the Army. They have spent the summer drinking and smoking dope.

Mark and Frank spent the early afternoon at Blatt State Park on the beach, where they smoked a couple joints out of the new batch of Jamaican that had just hit Oakridge. Later they went water skiing with a friend of Mark's. Now at the Grotto, showered and feeling the sunburn through their t-shirts, the cold beer is going down easy.

"Hey," Mark says. "You want to go to the party out at the country club?"

"Sure," Frank says and pictures what he thinks it might look like since he has never been there.

At 7:30 pm at the country club pool, Jean Holz, wearing her new, two-piece bathing suit, climbs out of the pool near the diving boards. Her figure is full and taut, and she appreciates the many male glances she receives. Henry Trumbull, the country club drunk, has just come out of the men's room holding his perpetual double gin. His eyes widen at the sight of the deeply tanned woman before him. Before Jean can protest, he has his arm around her shoulders and has pulled her close. "Say, haven't we met before?"

Jean humors him, trying to work her way loose. "Henry! You aren't stewed already!"

"No. Quit drinking. Bad for my liver, the doctor says. Just drink this special water that fellow in the white coat gives me," he says, holding his drink up before her. "Come on, I'll show you my new Cadillac." He pulls her along the pool toward the exit.

Someone yells, "Henry, you've got the wrong woman again!" Laughter greets the joke. Alice Trumbull looks across the pool at her wayward husband. She wouldn't come to the parties here at the club if it weren't that Henry always needs someone to drive him home. He wrecked a car a few years before, just missed a tree, and she knows it will happen again if she isn't with him.

Henry's hand slips down around Jean's waist. She doesn't like his pawing and jerks away. There is a shout, and the partiers turn to watch Jean and Henry tumble into the pool.

Chapter 2

Mark and Frank crack the first bottle of a six pack of Boone's Farm Apple wine on the way to the country club. They trade the bottle back and forth, the purr of the flathead 8 from Frank's '51 Ford pickup mixing with the humming sound of hard tires on warm asphalt. Warm air flows through the cab: sweet, pungent with the sap of hay, with the faint trailings of cow manure. The cold wine tastes good.

They pass Blatt State Park and approach the country club. "Want to run over and see my uncle?" Frank asks.

"Sure. No hurry to get to the party. Don't need to go at all."

A mile past the club Frank turns down a dusty, gravel road. "Ever been out to Hillman's trailer camp?" Frank asks, cracking open another bottle of Boone's Farm Apple.

"No." But Mark has heard of the place, which serves as a sort of check-in point for Kentuckians and West Virginians seeking work.

"My uncle just got in last week. Staying with a friend out here. He had to try something. Nothing down home anymore."

They pull onto a rutted, dirt lane and follow a dry creek bed. They round a curve and Mark sees a haphazard grouping of house trailers, decaying automobiles, and a fairly new Cadillac. A black and tan hound stands in the roadway barking at them. Children in the creek bed stop their play and watch Frank's truck. A three story farm house sits dead center at the end of the lane.

"Know why hillbillies live in house trailers?" Frank asks.

"No," Mark says, curious.

"The mine companies control near all of the land down home. So most folks have to rent land and park wherever they can. Then when the mine company gets ready to strip where the trailers are, all the folks do is haul their trailers to their next parking place. Used to be, people would build on the land they leased. That's how my folks ended up here in Oakridge. They'd built a place; Dad did all the work himself."

"They had a lease written up for five years at a time and never heard much from the company that owned the land, just sent their lease money in every three months. Then one spring a company man came around and told us they were getting ready to strip that section. They started digging out all around us and on the mountain. After a few weeks Dad saw it wasn't any use trying to stay there. We could barely get into the house anymore, the way they were dozing all around it. Tore Dad up, having to leave his house behind. So we came up here. Never knew that, did you?" Frank, watching the grave look on Mark's face, laughs a bellowing laugh. "Never knew what you were missing up here in Oakridge." He punches Mark's shoulder, and Mark drops the bottle.

Then they are both laughing as Mark scrambles to grab for the bottle on the seat.

"No need to worry about things," Frank says. "It's every man for himself. No need to feel guilty about anything in America."

Frank parks beside an ancient, green, lopsided Plymouth. Traces of white paint are still evident on the mostly grayed boards of the house. The three men on the porch stop playing. One has a banjo, another a mandolin, and the other a fiddle. Frank stands beside the truck. "Get that music rollin'!"

"How're ya, Frank," calls the one with the banjo. "Just warmin' up. There's another fellow bringing his guitar yet."

Luke is slender, tall like all the men in his family. His arms seem too thin against the rest of his body, but betray wire-like muscles.

"Just stopped by to say hello," Frank says. "Want some wine?"

"No. Quit drinkin' it. Hurts my head."

"This is Mark."

"Jimmy and Jacob," Luke says, motioning to the other men. "Get yourself a beer," Luke says, pointing to the twelve pack on the porch railing.

"Can't stay long. Just stopped to see if you'd found any work yet."

"I surely did. Standard Oil Company in Cranston. Pays better than I thought I'd find. Startin' me off at $2.50 an hour."

The screen door swings open, and two women step onto the porch. "Cool out here with the breeze," the pregnant one says. Jimmy and Jacob vacate their stools for the ladies.

"Never met my wife, did you, Frank?" Luke asks.

"Never did. Didn't know you had two of them, though."

The women laugh, and the pregnant one turns to face Frank as Luke names her. "This is Elly."

"Hi," she says shyly.

"How'd you ever talk such a pretty girl into marrying

you?" Frank asks Luke.

"You talk like your daddy," Elly says. "Always kiddin'." She is pretty, with brownish-blond hair and a brightness to her cheeks. "You even look like him a lot, big like he is. Your daddy's one of the biggest men I ever seen."

The guitar player arrives and sits on the railing. The banjo takes the lead with a running pattern, the mandolin folds in its delicate harmony, then the guitar and fiddle join. The music is mellow, smooth, exciting in its rapid pattern.

Sitting on a rotting porch step, Mark gazes down the lane. The sun is setting, hidden by the hill that rises beyond the creek bed. People are sitting on the metal-grate steps of their trailers or on kitchen chairs along the driveway. Several children are still playing in the smooth-pebbled creek, skipping stones in the puddles left from the last rain. A small boy runs up to the porch and stands staring at Mark. Others come, drawn by the music. The tune ends, and in the distance, from one of the trailers, comes the crash of breaking glass and a woman's shrieking voice.

"That'd be the Lawsons," Jimmy says. "Leavin' for down home in the mornin'."

Then the music is there again, overriding whatever the Lawsons are struggling with, filtering its melody into the woods. Frank tries one song with the banjo, but Luke tells him he sucks and takes the instrument again. They sit playing song after song until the mosquitoes come in swarms and the daylight is nearly lost. Frank stands up and finishes his beer. "If you need anything, let me know."

"Thank ya, Frank."

Then the old pickup is bouncing back toward the gravel road, raising a thin cloud of dust which settles over the trailers. In a couple minutes they pull off the highway onto the long, paved driveway of the country club. As they crest the hill, they can see the lights at the pool, and as they draw closer can hear laughter and music. Frank parks next to the cornfield that crowds close to the wood fence of the pool area.

Mark is brooding, feels he owes something somewhere to somebody, but can't pinpoint anything— only has this vague feeling of guilt. Frank lights a joint and hands it to him, laughing. "Last one. We better get rid of it."

They pass the weed back and forth, its heavy, thick smoke curling out the windows of the truck. The corn stalks stand whispering beside them, and the dense, pollen-laden air is tinged with chlorine.

Chapter 3

"Phew," Mark gasps. The door swings out, creaking as metal grinds on rusting metal within the ancient hinge. Frank laughs, "Getting it on tonight."

They water corn stalks. "Helps the corn grow. You know, a little last minute fertilizer."

Frank leads the way in, taking long lumbering strides, swinging the carton of Boone's Farm in a wide arc at his side. He's buzzed from the wine and weed, and as often happens when he is stoned out, he's in the mood to fuck with people. When Mark has caught up, Frank is shaking the hand of the first man who turned to look at him. "How're ya tonight, old buddy?" Frank says.

"Fine. How're you?"

"Real good. Great. Fine evening!"

"Didn't catch the name," the man says now, surveying the towering frame before him, the half-buttoned western shirt, faded jeans, suede boots.

"Frank."

"Last name?"

"Don't need no last name on Saturday nights. You got a name or shall I just call you Shorty?"

"Uh, Carl," he laughs as he turns away and nudges the man next to him.

Frank pushes his way onward, shaking hands with anyone who turns to look at him. "Hi," he says to John Holz. "Frank's my name. I'm in shipping," Mark hears.

John turns to his son. "Who is this?"

"Frank Baker, like you to meet my dad." The two shake hands again, Frank laughing. Then John is laughing.

Mark and Frank move around the pool, looking for a place to park themselves. Frank winks at a middle-aged woman, scrunching up the side of his face in comic exaggeration. She laughs and looks to the others at her table, then turns and watches Frank moving along the walkway shaking hands with anyone in his path.

They find an empty table and sit down to watch the festivities. Mark sees Amy Blatt approaching their table with Karen Blair. Amy looks beautiful to him as she has since they were children together. Her family and his were always close with their shared interest in the metal works.

"We were sitting here," she says.

Mark looks around as if seeking another table where he and Frank might sit. "You can stay here," she laughs. "We were by ourselves."

In a few moments the girls are seated across from each other. Frank takes a swig from the bottle, a long gurgling drink, wipes his mouth on his hairy forearm, and asks Mark, "Which one you want?"

Karen pushes her chair back. Amy looks at Frank. "You can't gross us out. So don't bother to try." Then she looks closely at him. "You're Frank...Frank Kruger. You were a couple years ahead of us at school."

"Frank's right. Not even close on the last name." He takes another swallow of wine.

"I'm sorry," she says laughing. "Haven't seen you since high school. You were in the army, weren't you?"

"Marines. Don't seem to remember you, though. What's your name?"

She is exasperated. "Come on. Quit putting us on, or we'll go find another table." Karen nods agreement.

"Okay, sure. You're Amy Bratt, the cheerleader."

"First name's right. Okay, we're even. Now what are you guys doing? This is a swim party. Where're your suits?"

Frank stands up and starts to unbuckle his pants. "Go ahead," Karen says. "Let's see if everything else is as big as your mouth."

Frank sits back down. "Hard woman. Wouldn't want to frighten you ladies. Want some wine?" he asks holding the bottle of apple wine toward Karen. She accepts it and takes a healthy swallow, as does Amy when the bottle is handed to her.

"Here. Drink out of these glasses," a middle-aged woman tells them and sets several respectable, plastic tumblers on the table.

"Oh, Mother. It all tastes the same," Amy says.

"Mark! Where have you been all summer?" Mrs. Blatt addresses him.

"Been working this year. Not playing much golf."

"And you're so good at it. That's a shame."

When she has gone, they resume their conversation. Amy asks Mark how college has gone. "It went all right, didn't flunk out or anything. But I'm not going back."

"Not going back?" There is surprise and concern in her voice. "What will you do?"

"Might learn a trade. Dig ditches."

"What do you do?" Karen asks Frank.

"I'm in shipping now," he says.

"Really?" She is impressed. "Do you have your own business?"

"Not yet. Might go in partners with Mark here."

Mark is laughing. "Yeah, you can have the left side of the dock, and I'll take the right."

They laugh and open another bottle of wine. Frank takes it and chugs, comes up for air, and lets out a deep-throated belch. "You're crazy," Amy says in wonderment. "Why do you want to get so drunk?"

Frank starts to answer but realizes he doesn't know.

The girls take off their robes and head for the pool.

Mark and Frank stay at the table, occasionally silencing the people at the neighboring tables with their laughter.

After a while Jean Holz can be seen making her way through the crowd of people.

"Check this out," Frank says to Mark, who glances up and sees her coming towards them, still wearing her new bathing suit. She stops at the table next to them to talk to its occupants. Mark winks at Frank and walks over to the table. Grasping her elbow, he says something to her, and she turns and sits down across from Frank. He reaches the green bottle to her. "Like some wine?"

Mark resumes his seat. "Mom, this is Frank Baker." Frank leans back laughing.

"What's so funny?" she asks.

"Frank thought, Frank was admiring your bathing suit, and he didn't know who you were."

She smiles at Frank, then turns to Mark. "Honey, why don't you get me a collins. I'm nearly exhausted from swimming."

"Sure."

"You boys have been attracting quite a lot of attention over here tonight."

"Well, we offer some of our wine to anybody who comes around. Just because we've got all the good liquor is no reason for folks...."

Jean laughs. "Are you serious? That has to be the

worst. What's it cost? A dollar a bottle?"

"Dollar and a quarter. Price went up. It's cheap but gives you a good buzz." Frank grins and winks, mock insanity on his face.

Mark returns with the drink. "Mom, you and Frank ought to have a lot in common," he says as he sits down. "He reads a lot like you do."

"Really," she says, takes a sip of the foam-topped drink and looks at Frank. "What sort of things do you read?"

"Oh, just about anything. Don't read like I used to when I was in the service."

"Who are your favorite authors?"

He takes a swig from the bottle. "Hard to pin it down. Kesey, or Tolkien. Dostoyevsky."

They talk books for a couple of minutes, Frank's thoughts drifting back and forth between Dostoyevsky's vision of God and man and Jean's breasts. When Frank declares that James Joyce's work is worthless, Jean gets up and leaves.

Others come to see Mark and Frank, slowly, with dignity, as if they are coming to an especially interesting exhibit in a museum. Karen and Amy return after a while with a huge platter of sloppy joes. Frank eats the first sandwich quickly, then another. He keeps eating, occasionally smiling a tomato sauce-smeared grin at the girls, who are not doing well at hiding their disgust.

A loud speaker cuts through the festivities, and Jerry Shunk, the owner and editor of the *Oakridge Chronicle,* stands on the low diving board. "May I have your attention!" Silence replaces the revelry. "As you all know, the *Oakridge Chronicle* puts out a special edition every two years: 'Who's Who in Oakridge.' Normally the edition doesn't come out until after Labor Day, but this year it is coming out early." An undercurrent of low voices and whispers arises from the crowd.

Having heard his cue, a man comes through the gate carrying a bundle of papers. He wears a dark t-shirt and the ink smudges of a pressman. Embarrassed, he hangs back near the gate until the loud speaker silences the crowd, and their attention is once again on Jerry.

"We can be proud of the prosperity that has always been our heritage in Oakridge. From the time the last of the Indians were driven from the forests of Ohio, Oakridge has in one way or another contributed to the well-being of this great country, and thereby helped to preserve the freedom that we all enjoy and often take for granted. We are an industrial town, not large, but I think unique. In miniature, we have the best that is to be found in this great country."

"Bullshit," Frank says. "Half the people I know are out of work."

"What we attempt to do in our publication of 'Who's Who in Oakridge' is to credit those to whom credit is due—the men and women who make possible our excellent industries, churches and schools. Many would criticize these people today, saying things out of ignorance or hatred or jealousy. But we in Oakridge will not bow to these passing fancies of what is right and wrong. Those who are willing to work and who persevere are those who prosper here. The least we can do to repay our leaders in these trying times is to honor them as they deserve to be honored, make it known that we respect them. Hopefully, our newspaper's humble effort to accomplish these purposes will help our traditions to endure."

Jerry lowers the microphone, and the people stand and clap and cheer. He stands before them for a few moments, enjoying their applause, then raises his hand for silence. "The special edition will be beside the bar."

The people amble along toward the bar, trying not to seem too eager to find out who has been chosen for this special honor. And shortly they are seeking out their esteemed leaders, most of whom are at the party, shaking their hands, slapping their backs, and expressing their respect.

But cries from the end of the pool draw attention. Frank stands on the diving board holding his arms up in a huge V. The people gather around, laughing and pointing to the actor on the board.

"And verily, I say unto you," Frank is shouting, doing his Cotton Mather imitation, "that *we* are the chosen people, that *we* have been chosen to lead the flock out of ignorance, pestilence, flood and famine. And like Abraham we shall reap the rewards of our labors, forever fighting the elements in the world that would lead us to sin."

Henry Trumbull makes his way up the two steel steps and walks slowly onto the board, holding his arms out at his sides, concentrating to keep his balance and at the same time keep from spilling his drink.

"Oakridge is the chosen city, the new Jerusalem," Frank shouts. Feeling the presence on the board, he turns to see Henry behind him grinning. He puts his arm around Henry's shoulders and draws him forward. "And here is our saviour."

Henry stands grinning and holding his plastic tumbler heavenward, then takes a short bow, bumping Frank. The two men struggle to regain their balance, teetering back and forth hopefully. Frank's booming laugh is smothered by the clean, green water.

Chapter 4

Murmurs of conversation ring the pool in a sort of monotone. "What was that all about?" "Who the hell is that?" "What was he saying?" But those who heard the mimic from the onset are silent, waiting expectantly.

John Holz stands with Mark. "That dumbass." Mark looks to his father's tightened face.

Frank erupts from the deep end of the pool in a shower of spray and foam, blowing out a mouthful of water with a snort; and then, like a great, untamed animal—from the sea, maybe, just evolving from an aquatic existence—starts splashing through the country club pool with great, flopping butterfly strokes, the chlorine-filtered water boiling along beside him, splashing onto the cement perimeter, waves breaking in all directions. Silent now, they stand and watch the creature, its huge arms churning the water violently as he makes his way through their regulation, Olympic-size pool. Mark is laughing, unable to stop the surge from within, and by the time Frank is half way down the pool, others join Mark's lead, laughing uncontrollably as they begin to sense the absurdity of what is happening. One small group near the shallow end even applauds as Frank pulls himself out of the pool. At the other end, Henry, out of the pool now, is dancing a stumbling jig.

Bill Blatt and Gary Cooper stand midway along the pool, clutching their plastic tumblers. "Ought to throw the bastard out."

Gary nods in agreement, "He's a big son-of-a bitch, though." Bill narrows his eyes at the creature as it laughs its booming laugh.

The hilarity of the people wells up, grows until Frank's laugh is obliterated. They cheer and laugh, not knowing why.

Mark slips away from John and heads toward Frank.

Frank grins and flexes his chest and arms, shaking off the water like a bear after salmon fishing. The dip has sobered him up. "I think it's time to split." They look around and receive enough menacing glares that Mark readily agrees.

"Yeah, right. You okay to drive?"

"Sure."

"I'm sticking around. Want to talk to Amy."

"Max is having a party tonight. We still going?"

"Meet you there," Mark says.

Mark looks at the men by the pool. They might be like the group that hanged the black from the New York Central crossing gate in 1900 in uptown Oakridge, or like the mass of townsmen and farmers who hunted down a would-be bank robber in '31 and killed him, only to find that the desperado was a fifteen-year-old kid from their own countryside.

"Works at National Carton," Mark hears someone say from the midst of the committee as he walks by. Finding out Frank's identification, Mark thinks, getting ready to do what? Mark sits down with Amy, trying to quell the surge of adrenalin that is inciting him to action of some sort. He wishes he had not stayed, that he had gone with Frank.

"That was beautiful," Amy says, laughing. "Nobody's ever told them how stupid these newspaper awards are."

Mark is surprised. "I didn't think you were

appreciating it."

"We probably had it coming. You know how it was in high school, all of us with our own little groups, the jocks and cheerleaders, the cliques. Frank was always on the outside of all that."

"You're right. But he's beyond all that stuff. He has this philosophy that all things are related to the earth. Our relationship to the earth is now indirect, not direct as it once was. We ride in cars instead of walking, buy food in cans and cardboard, buy clothes, houses, buy all the things families used to make for themselves."

"But we can't go back in time. That's crazy."

"The philosophy doesn't say we should do anything. It's like a," the word comes slowly, "a mourning for what was. We don't really have any choice in the matter. Since the relationship is indirect now, we have this huge hierarchy of society and industry and everything; property is not distributed according to a person's efforts, but by who you know, how much money your parents have, and so most of our modern-day problems are related to this hierarchy. Why should the family or society survive if none of its members need each other?"

Karen comes to join them at the table as Mark pursues his train of thought. "When I was about sixteen, I used to look forward to the day when I would be older, I figured by now anyway, when everything would be different, when we would all be grown up and living in a comprehensible world. But it gets worse as you get older. We all seem to get stuck deeper and deeper in the ruts we've been in all our lives."

"What are you talking about?" Karen breaks in.

"About the state of the world."

"We're going to solve the sociological slights of

Oakridge," Amy says and laughs a short laugh, brushing her long, dark hair back.

"Good luck."

"Let's get out of here for a while," Mark says.

"Where?"

Mark glances around. "Anywhere, outside the pool, go for a walk or something. There's a party in town."

Amy gets up and fastens her jacket. Karen stays there, saying she has to get home early with her folks.

As they walk out the gate they are enveloped by the fading humidity and gentle cooling of the late summer evening. The warmth of the day is lifted by the dew, and the sounds—the crickets chirping their continual chorus of night, the squeaking bats buzzing the pool's brightness, the frogs at the pond on the ninth hole—all blend together to orchestrate the patterns of existence.

"Where are we going?" she asks as they reach the edge of a fairway.

"I don't know."

In the distance a pair of headlights pierce the darkness. "Who's that, I wonder?" she asks.

'The greenskeeper. Turning off the sprinklers."

"I never knew he worked at night."

"Jim doesn't mind. He just lives down the road and says it gives him a good excuse to get out of the house when he wants to."

They walk on, the moon casting a silver tint on the world now that they are away from the artificial brightness of the pool lights. "How come you're not going back to school?"

"It just doesn't feel right for some reason. I guess I've changed a lot over the last year."

"What's that got to do with educating yourself?"

"Maybe that's it. I'm *not* educating myself. You're not either, if you really stop to think about it."

"Who else is educating me?" she laughs.

"Well, you're doing the learning part, but you can learn all you want without going to school. A college degree is something you buy, and neither one of us is footing the bill. Last winter when I had Mom's car at school before Christmas, I stopped at this gas station next to campus. I had Dad's credit card and everything, and this guy who was in my religion class, a pretty smart guy, you know, always carrying on a conversation between himself and the professor and a couple of other brains, came out to wait on me. He didn't say anything, just put in the gas and checked the oil. Then he wrote up the bill and stamped the credit card. I signed for it and started the car. You know what he said?"

She shrugs.

"He said, 'Here, don't forget Daddy's credit card.' It made me mad. I had a date and everything, and here's this guy saying this and making out that I'm just a little boy. But I've thought about it. He was right. I was just a little boy playing college. This guy's pumping gas every night and paying his own way."

"But you can't think that way. Without having to work all the time you have more time to spend on your studies."

"Aw, come on. You know as well as I do that it doesn't take long to do the work. I never spent much time studying."

"I guess you're right," she says, pondering something which she has never let enter her conscious mind. "Maybe you just don't know what you want to do."

"That's for sure," he laughs.

"That might be the problem. I doubt I would stay in school if I didn't know what I wanted to do."

"What would that be?"

"Teaching developmentally disabled kids. Junior high age."

She takes his hand. "Remember when we were kids how we used to hold hands and run and jump into our swimming pool?"

"Yeah," he says, this delightful thought flooding over him. "Spent hours running and jumping."

They both run, laughing to accompany this thought buried so many years ago to make way for new things. But after twenty yards they stop.

The breeze rustles the corn plants, as if there were a lot of whispering going on, nature breathing her gentle secrets to the fields and animals. Shiny green stalks of corn reflect silver from the moon.

They end up in the cornfield, following a row ten rows into the field, and away from the golf course. They come upon the little grave yard that they know is there in the middle of the cornfield and sink down onto the grassy area surrounding the three head markers.

She wonders as he kisses her why they never got together before. He is thinking similar. It feels right to both of them.

They are quiet as they dress a while later and walk back out of the field.

Chapter 5

Amy and Mark are still silent on the drive to town. Tonight was different from any she has ever experienced. She wonders how it was before civilization, before factories and towns, how it would be: violent, maybe, or perhaps gentle and wild as tonight in the field—or maybe more permanent than she can imagine, with a strong, knotty-muscled man keeping her for himself, fighting to the death should another tamper with his woman or family.

Mark tells her where to turn as they reach Oakridge. They pass a few homes, and a little way further is a field bordering the metal works steel yard. Set by itself in the field is an old two story farm house. Amy parks at the end of the driveway behind a double line of a dozen or so cars.

When they step onto the long, wooden porch they can feel the waves of sound, feel the porch boards rattling.

"They have a band here?" she asks in surprise.

"I don't think Max planned on enough of the people showing up, but I guess they did."

"What people?"

"Somebody has a party and it turns into a jam—everybody who plays brings his instrument along and they just play all evening, jam together. You remember Max, don't you?"

"He's a year older than us, if I'm thinking of the right guy. Used to play the saxophone in the concert band at school."

"Right. He played bass with the Tale-Enders. They

had one good song that some of the Columbus and
Cleveland stations played, but they couldn't get off the
ground after that."

He pulls open the screenless door, and they step into
a smoke and people-filled room. The music is deafening,
and Amy covers her ears and turns in surprise to Mark.
In front of them a pale girl with stringy blond hair sits
Indian-style, rocking absently back and forth. As Mark
looks around the room for a little open space he and
Amy might utilize, someone hands him a joint. He grins
and takes a hit and hands it to Amy. On the couch lies an
exceedingly thin boy with curly, black hair. His mouth
is lopsidedly open, and he is gone for the night. In the
next room the band is wailing away. Nobody is talking,
since the music is so loud. As Mark leads Amy across
the room, a girl stands up and hands Mark a pipe with at
least a gram of hash already toked up. He takes a big
pull of the stuff, nods his head and widens his eyes as
the taste confirms that it's first class, and passes it on.

A child, who looks to be about three years old, darts
in front of Amy into the other room, where he stops next
to one of the guitar amplifiers and sits down to play with
the electric cord. An older boy wearing Bert and Ernie
pajamas stands on the staircase rubbing his eyes and
searching the room.

To Amy's relief, the band stops playing. The
musicians put their instruments down and slap each
other's hands in applause for their performance. Mark
takes Amy's hand, and they get through the room as
others come to play and instruments are switched. By
the time they have reached the kitchen, the lead guitar is
already twanging a random few notes, and a very fat girl
is tapping out an introduction on the hundred dollar

piano.

Frank stands in the kitchen with a girl almost as tall as he is, his arm slung loosely around her bony shoulders. Max is at the plywood counter making a plate of gooey peanut butter and jelly sandwiches. "Hey, what's happenin'?" he calls to Mark.

"Good party."

"About like the one we just left," Frank says.

"Got to give the kids a snack. They can't sleep for a while yet," Max says and motions at the stack of sandwiches.

"Finally made it," Frank says, his eyes glistening, obviously working up to a repeat performance for the night. "Here, look what Helen scrounged up for us." He reaches inside the pocket of her blue work shirt and comes out holding four hearts in the palm of his hand.

"Damn! Thought they quit making those."

The band is tuning up in the other room, every instrument manned again by someone. Mark takes a couple of the pills, pops them into his mouth and washes them down with a beer. Amy makes a face as Mark offers her one. "What are they?"

Frank intervenes before Mark can explain. "These, young lady, are the elixir of the middle-class, suburban housewife. By taking one of these every morning she can be sure that the house is spotless, the clothes washed, food cooked. With one of these tiny pills and a full pot of coffee the ordinary lady of the homestead is miraculously transformed into a dynamo of energy. There is no task too large for her to undertake."

Amy is feeling more than a little insulted and out of place, and besides that, she has to go the bathroom.

"You fucker," Mark says, "you're speeding your

brains out. How many of those things did you eat?"

"That's entirely irrelevant to the situation at hand. You see, we are only alive for this moment. There is no past unless we allow our minds to search for it, or perhaps all we are is the past. Maybe we are the embodiment of all experiences we have had from birth. There is also no future, unless we allow our minds to think of it. Then, of course, you might say that all there is is the future, that if man does not have a host of false hopes to carry him from day to day, if he does not plan or wish certain things to happen, then he will lose the will to live and do away with himself. Like the lemmings, maybe, only we go about it more gradually with booze, cigarettes, and yes, last but not least, the great god speed, designed to burn away the fat of secretary spread, flabby tummies, and make us all thin and svelte. Svelte," Frank repeats the word. "That's neat. *Svelte* is a neat word. Sounds Russian. Look out! Commie words are infiltrating our language!" Then comes the bellowing laugh. Max picks up the plate of sandwiches as the boy in Bert and Ernie pajamas approaches from the other room, puts his hand on the boy's head, and steers him toward the stairway beyond the band.

Max is quickly back in the kitchen holding the hand of the younger boy who was playing in front of the guitar amp. The boy is crying huge tears and sucking on the fingers of his free hand.

"That stupid Wilson. Gets all downed out and tries to give a joint to him," he says as he bends down and pulls the boy's hand out of his mouth. There is a huge blister on his finger. "That's all right; let's put some cream on it," Max says, standing up and opening the cupboard. He applies the salve and tells the boy to run upstairs where there is a treat waiting for him.

With the constant traffic of people pushing past her to get to the refrigerator and the deafening sounds of the band, Amy is growing more uncomfortable. She asks Max where the bathroom is and begins making her way to the stairs, past the band and the few still conscious enough to dance, stepping carefully through the people sitting on the floor. She feels relieved when she has reached the relative quiet of the upstairs, where three children are playing with Tonka trucks and eating sandwiches.

On she goes, enters the bathroom, and closes the door. She searches for a few moments for a latch of some kind, but cannot find one. Suddenly the door swings open and a bearded stranger calls, "Anybody in here?"

She kicks the door, kicks for all she's worth, and he backs out quickly. As she flushes the john she can hear him mumbling in the hallway to himself. But when she is outside, there is no one there.

She heads for the stairs, stopping for a moment to watch the children. Downstairs the band is blaring feverishly, the joints moving around the room. Before the coffee table by the couch the sickly, pale girl is snorting some white powder through a rolled up dollar bill.

Amy stands at the bottom of the stairs, then heads for the door. Enough is enough, she tells herself as she starts her car. She backs out quickly and jams the shifter into drive. She's angry at Mark for bringing her here and feels badly that her tender feelings have been betrayed.

Mark is involved in conversation, the speed just

beginning to hit him, before he realizes that Amy is gone. He searches for her in the house and, finding no sign of her, goes outside and down the drive before he sees that her car is gone. He will have to make it up to her later.

Back inside, Frank is mock-dancing, bending his gangly frame, grotesquely missing the beat, standing before the bass player, mocking him, mocking them, mocking himself, humankind, it's past and present rules, mocking the universe, daring it to reveal itself to him.

The bass player leans his guitar against the wall, and in a few moments the others have stopped playing. Frank dances on. "Who the hell you think you are?" he finally says to Frank.

Frank roars his laugh and bends over, grabs the bass player by the ankles and jerks him off his feet to hold him upside down. He holds him dangling there for a few moments, then lets him down gently. His victim stares up at Frank from his hands and knees, thankful that he had not taken a swing at him.

The music starts again, and Mark is getting into it now, his mind racing beyond his body. With another beer, he settles back against the wall. There is strength surging through his limbs, a feeling of can-do-anything and the temporary happiness of the speed trip. He feels the cold dampness in his armpits and bums a cigarette, then settles into the wall itself, feels the old horsehair plaster envelop him as thoughts race through his mind.

And this certain room comes to Mark's mind, this secret room he occasionally dreams about, waking and knowing he has been there, lived there in some life. He sees it clearly—the second story flat with peeling wallpaper, crusted dust on the floor and in the corners.

An ugly, pale green room.

Frank is in the kitchen with Helen, telling her about the mountain, talking a mile a minute, laughing, visualizing how he wants it to be; this log cabin, he is saying, on the side of the mountain, and a view of an Appalachian valley, a virgin forest to calm one's spirit, a vastness only nature can possess—the land, and he is into his spiel, telling all about it for maybe the hundredth time, always coming back to it, always keeping his vision of what he wants and how he wants it, sharing this vision, hoping that someday he can do it, make it happen and not join the rest of the lemmings in their plunge to death.

And the music is there, folks jamming with one another, practicing for themselves, each person sitting tight in his own little world, drifting to wherever the pot and hash lead, following the snort of coke or THC or junk to its ultimate high, the speed and mescaline turning minds inside out so that there may be at least a temporary semblance of peace, the beer and whiskey doing all it has ever done, bringing on aggression and sickness, and the wine along with the grass—that's not so bad—a good buzz, and on and on into the night in this ramshackle house in the field, on into the morning it lasts, and bodies cover the floor, passed out or just sleeping, and on it goes, the house in the field still as after a storm, the town of Oakridge waking to the tolling of church bells, the farmers waking to their harvest duties

Chapter 6

Mark turns in his sleep, the morning sun pushing through his bedroom window, forcing him to a lighter stage of sleep. And there is that room again, up the stairs, steep stairs as would be found in a very old tenement – like Europe, maybe – yes, somewhere Mark has never seen, since this time he sees that there are cobblestones on the street. For a moment he hears the clopping of horses' hooves and he is upstairs in the apartment again, the ugly green, the green of mold and rot and sickness pervading all corners of the room. Peeling wallpaper appears as it has always appeared, and the room is bare as if no one ever lived there, no furniture, no source of warmth or feeling of home. And then from the room where he sits gazing down at the horses on the cobblestone lane, Mark hears shouting, thinking at first that it is only the wagon driver calling orders to his horses. But no, there are two voices, and there is fear as there is so often in his dreams and visions of the room, and in the fear he tosses and turns, the agony and angry voices coupled with the sunlight finally forcing him awake.

He still hears the angry voices but finds himself sitting up in his own bed – no green room anymore – just his home in Oakridge, his own room and his desk and color television and his bed and the plush carpeting and wood paneling. He tries to remember more about the green room, tries to remember and add details to the scene.

"Well," Mark hears his father shout, "What did you

expect me to do? Come right over to the two of you and say, 'Hey that's my wife you're fooling around with?' Did you expect me to punch him in the nose?"

"But Jerry's your best friend. And my friend. How can you think such a thing?"

"I know what I saw, best friend or not."

"John, you're acting crazy."

The speed is working on Mark, cutting through the drowsiness he talked himself into only a few hours before, and he has the shakes. He steps into his shoes, needing a cup of coffee.

"Come on," Mark says as he enters the kitchen and heads for the coffee pot, ready to assume his regular role as peace-maker. Usually he is able to make his parents realize how stupid and unnecessary their arguments are.

"Come on, hell," John says, sitting up straight, the anger once again controlling him.

"You embarrassed me in front of a lot of people last night, people I've known for years coming up and asking me who was the idiot you brought with you, and you two sitting around drinking all that cheap wine. I want some answers."

Jean sees another chance to get even. "He wasn't really an idiot. He knows a lot about books and writers. All you know how to do is work."

John groans. "I don't care if he was Davinsky himself, or whoever it is you've been reading about. He's a redneck punk and didn't belong out there last night."

"And what is wrong with work?" John says. "I've given over twenty years of my life to provide this," and he gestures with both arms to indicate the home and its fine trappings, "and you criticize me?"

John rounds on Mark again. "You knew all along what was happening last night."

"I didn't know anything," Mark says, the coffee already working with the leftover amphetamine to clear his mind. "Besides, a lot of people thought he was pretty funny. All he really did was make a few people laugh. Some of those fogies out there haven't had a good gut laugh like that for years."

"Funny? Making fun of something that has been a tradition in this town for fifty years is funny?" The sadness comes to John, and he rubs his eyes and forehead as if massaging away his anger. "Well, I don't want to go on with this. Can't even talk to my family any more. You'll be going back to school in a few days, back to the friends who are really going to matter and be valuable to you," John says to Mark, as if to conclude the argument.

"I'm not going back to school," Mark says.

"What?"

"I'm not going back to school."

John half laughs and groans, not taking Mark seriously. "What do you think you're going to do, live here the rest of your life?"

"I can move out now if you want me to. I've got a job. I can pay my own way."

"Why can't you go back?" Jean asks. "Has something happened that you need to tell us about?"

"If I could tell you I would, but I don't know what it is myself."

"But you're going to miss so much if you don't go," Jean says. "*I'm* going back to school this fall. Aren't there things you want to learn?"

John looks to his wife. *"You* are? You haven't said

anything about it for months."

"You know I decided for sure last spring."

Mark looks tiredly from one parent to the other. "I just can't do it now. I'll flunk out."

John slams his fist onto the table. "You are going and that's all there is to it."

Mark stands up. "You can't tell me what to do any more. I don't have to stand here and listen to you."

Calmly, as if a solution has come to him, John says, "You're going to school whether you like it or not. We'll see about your job. It could end any day."

"I'll start moving out this afternoon."

John looks at his watch. "I've got to get going. Got an early tee time."

Mark and his mother are still sitting at the table when John leaves for the golf course.

"Can't you tell me about it?" Jean asks, seeing painfully the developing depth and sensitivity of her only child. He doesn't answer, and she studies his fatigued face. He shakes his head no and holds back his feelings. "I wish it were that simple, Mom. I wish I could tell you something and be done with it."

Jean puts her arm around his shoulders and draws him close. "All right. Whatever you decide."

"I just need a little time to think my way through things."

She nods, a headache coming on, but manages a smile. "Settled, but don't move out yet. Give it a while. Please?"

He sits thinking. He doesn't really know where he would go if he were to move out. "Okay."

Jean pours herself another cup of coffee and walks into her library. From the drawer she takes two codeine tablets and washes them down. She looks over the computer forms for school, due this week. Quickly she decides on social stratification and creative writing, and fills out the proper spaces.

She sits looking to the woods as the brilliant day unfolds, feeling contented as the headache dissolves. She shuffles through the papers in the desk drawer—her journal, stories, and essays. Been writing since high school, publishing something now and then, just enough to make her believe she is good at it. It's frustrating for her though, not being able to make any real headway. She looks through the failed beginnings of the novel she started two years ago and drops it back in the drawer. Maybe with the writing course this fall she can get started on a novel. Hank Higby, the novelist who will be teaching the course, has three novels in print. He should be able to help. Strange, she thinks, that she has never really confided her ambitions to anyone. Just never sounded realistic, her wanting more than anything to complete a novel.

She gets a tablet out, wondering what she would be doing now if she had gone to New York as she had planned to do before she met John at college so many years ago. Sometimes she wishes she had gone, found a job with a publishing company and pursued her dreams, maybe failed at it, but at least she would know.

A scene from her childhood comes to mind and she records it as she remembers it:

> The leaves flashed brilliantly over the two young girls who lay on the rough boards of their tree house. The sun was out and it was a warm afternoon in the fall. They lay for some time,

pretending to be asleep. They were playing a game of living in the tree and in the game it was nighttime.

After they had lain this way for several minutes they heard a loud snort which frightened them. They looked at each other from where they lay, each afraid to move or talk. Then they could hear a rustling in the fallen leaves beneath the tree.

They inched their way to the edge so that they could see what was below them. They were surprised to see two large deer. One of the deer had antlers and he kept pawing the ground and moving around the other deer.

Jean puts the pen down and reads over what she has written. She sits pondering what should come next in the story but feels drowsy. Her thoughts turn away from the story and focus on her and John. Something has gone wrong with their relationship in the last several years. They have never argued the way they do now. Never abused each other so viciously. Eventually her thoughts lead her to the question that has lately been posing itself before her: Does she love John? No, she has to answer herself. But she's not sure. If only he were more tender with her, really showed he cared when they made love, or that he treasured her. She needs to feel loved again. They had loved once, had the best of things. But why the changes now? she asks herself. She wonders what it would be like to live again from payday to payday as they did when they first moved to Oakridge, her already pregnant with Mark. She looks around, and the two story brick home, symbol of their economic success, looks ridiculous to her. She's even tired of taking care of the place.

The phone rings. "Did I wake you?" Jerry Shunk asks.

"No, we've been up. Got an early start on the battlefield."

"Not again."

"Jerry, I just don't know anymore. I can't understand it. It just happens and there we are clawing away at each other."

"And you know what started it this morning?" she continues. "He thought you and I were being too friendly last night. He was actually angry with me, and with you too. But maybe it was just because you didn't put him in the 'Who's Who' thing."

"That's hard to believe. He actually thought that you and I…"

"It's crazy, isn't it?"

"Yeah. Maybe it *was* because of the newspaper awards. But that's really out of my control. You know, there's a committee to decide."

"I suppose it will pass. But you're one of the few people who really know me. I've got to be able to talk seriously with someone."

"Sure. And I understand. I always enjoy talking with you. So where's John?"

"He had an early tee time this morning."

"I was supposed to meet him at eleven. Maybe he's getting in an early round. I'll catch him at the club."

"Okay. See you later."

She dismisses the thoughts about John and reads over the beginning of the story again, changing a couple words and adding a comma. But her thoughts turn away from the story, this time to Mark and whatever troubles he is struggling with. After awhile, she showers, gets her bathing suit and tennis racket and leaves for the club.

Chapter 7

Mark laughs at Frank's joke with the others at the carton company. The whistle blows, marking the end of the break, and the men amble off to their jobs. Retrieving the broom he has been pushing all morning, Mark finds himself thinking of Amy again. How had he missed knowing her for so long? Grew up together and never realized she was as attracted to him as he had always felt to her.

He thinks of yesterday. He tried to call Amy all day, but couldn't reach her until evening. She agreed to see him then. After having pizza together, they drove out to the city reservoir and parked on the bank.

As the roar of the automated machinery fills the factory, Mark pictures the calmness, the water reflecting the slanted rays of the evening sun, no houses or highways in sight from where they parked. They talked, relaxing, laughing, learning more of each other's mature personalities and views. Dusk came and they watched the sun turn fiery red over the stand of oaks lining the banks. A few kisses then, and when darkness enveloped them, Mark took her home.

He remembers the kisses, the cornfield of Saturday night, remembers vividly and feels the stirring within, knows as he pushes the broom in the carton company that he is going to miss Amy. She is going back to school, to return to Oakridge at Thanksgiving probably, though she told him he might visit her or that she might plan to come home some weekend if he wanted her to. It feels good just to think of her. But he knows he can't see her very often, tells himself this and works a little faster as he sees his foreman approaching down the aisle.

John Holz leans back in his leather swivel chair surveying the paperwork amassed on his desk. He has to get to work, or he will have to take it home this evening. Mondays are his main day at the office, the day he lines up appointments for the rest of the week or services the accounts in his sales territory.

First he talks to Art Caldwell, the general manager at the carton company, about the United Appeal Fund. After ironing out the details for soliciting corporate contributions, John explains the situation of Mark and college, and they strike a deal on that: Caldwell will simply fire Mark so he has no choice but to return to school. And they plot for Frank, too. Caldwell was at the party Saturday night.

These matters cleared away, John picks out a couple of folders from the stack on his desk and gets down to work—sorting, remembering, calling credit or billing, checking inventories or lead time for new orders. By noon he has things under control and is able to take a long lunch with Jean.

After lunch, Mark and Frank are working hard, loading a drop shipment on a Roadway truck. Frank handles the fork lift while Mark does the paperwork, typing up the bill of lading for the driver to sign. He likes this part of the job, likes to occasionally be able to use his mind for its accuracy and quickness. But just as well, he likes climbing into a trailer and working it piece by piece.

They are nearly finished as the 1:30 break draws near. Frank is setting the last pallet inside the jammed van, nudging the pallets to get that last inch he needs to shut the door. Mark has already gotten the driver's signature and filed the paperwork in the shipping office.

Finished finally, with too little time to start some other project before break, they head down the aisle to wash up. As they near the washroom, Mark sees their foreman, Tony Edwards, coming toward them. Tony motions to them, and Mark waves back as they enter the enclosure.

But when they come out a couple of minutes later, Tony is waiting for them, looking worried about something. Again he motions to Mark and Frank, and he meets them in the aisle. He reaches in his shirt pocket, looking sheepish, like he wishes he were somewhere else, and pulls out two envelopes. He hands one to Mark and the other to Frank.

"What the hell's this?" Frank laughs. "You giving us a bonus 'cause we work so hard? About time."

They open their envelopes and see some papers inside. Mark pulls his out and looks at the check first, finding six days' pay on it. Then he looks at the pink slip, the Termination of Employment form from the office. Then Frank sees.

"Who you shitting?" Frank says.

Tony stands before them and shrugs. "It come out of the office. Caldwell gave 'em to me. I don't know what it's all about, but I have to do what he tells me." Tony shakes his head and turns away.

"Get my committeeman," Frank orders him.

In a few minutes the shop committeeman is on the

dock with them, looking over the forms. "They can't fire you," he tells Frank, then looks at Mark, "but they can fire you. You don't have your ninety days in yet. Big layoff coming anyway," he adds in consolation. Then he tells Frank, "We'll just shut the fucking place down. I'm not going to argue with Caldwell or any of those other fuckers today. They've been pushing too hard too long. They think 'cause work's slowing down we should kiss their ass to punch the timeclock."

By the time break is over word has spread, and they group in the parking lot to talk over the situation, coming to examine Frank's pink slip and talking among themselves about this blunder on the part of the company. Frank knows nearly all the workers in the place; and they know him, know his outgoing and friendly nature, and now they are willing to stand with him.

Mark knows he is out of a job no matter what the outcome of Frank's situation, but he can't understand the reason given on his pink slip: "Unsatisfactory work." He's always worked hard for Tony. And Frank's is just as ridiculous. "Excess absenteeism," his form says, but he has missed only three days in the last six months, well under the amount specified in the last contract concerning absences.

On the dock, several white shirts stand watching the group. The production manager is there along with the general foreman and a couple of line foremen. Soon Caldwell has joined them. They are concerned, since the first order of their new contract with a potato chip company is due to be shipped in three days. Someone throws a rock toward the men on the dock, and they make a hasty retreat. Some of the strikers are making picket signs to turn away the smaller second shift. Several whiskey bottles are making the rounds. "Too damn hot to work in there anyways," says one man. "Hell with 'em," says Sally Watson, one of the dozen women in the shop. "Burn the place down before we let 'em get away with this bullshit," another adds.

Mark suddenly knows why he and Frank were fired, remembers John's comment about his job. The adrenalin flows at the thought of confrontation with his father, and Mark finds himself growing agitated. He wants to punch someone or something, act upon his thought that his father had him and Frank fired. He has to do something, anything, towards resolving the urgency thrusting itself upon him. Mark tells Frank he'll meet him later at the Grotto and heads for his car.

Chapter 8

The thoughts come fast as Mark grips the steering wheel, his knuckles white from the pressure. Another voice is there also, a smaller voice of reason, telling him to slow down. But the voice of anger and adrenalin and emotion drowns out the smaller voice. Mark wheels into a reserved parking place before the brick front of Blatt Metal Works.

Then he is before the secretary, her IBM quiet now, the young woman startled at the slam of the door moments before, scared, wondering if maybe this is going to be like on television when people are held hostage by lunatic gunmen. But all there is in front of her is an agitated boy in soiled denims and t-shirt. "Whom did you wish to see?"

"John Holz. Where's John Holz?"

"He's in with Mr. Jordan now...but I don't believe he's expecting you."

In a moment he is at the door of the sales manager's office. He turns the knob and pushes, each movement conscious to him now as he is about to enter enemy territory. The door slams into the paneled wall of the office, and Mark sees his father, Gary Cooper, and Jordan seated around a large wooden table, all of them staring in disbelief at him.

"Why did you do it?" he demands, advancing towards his father. The men all stare dumbly. "Why would you do that to me?" Mark shouts.

John sits in amazement, then looks around to the other men. "Go wait in my office," he orders Mark.

John gets up and reaches for Mark's shoulders, meaning to grasp and steer him out of the office, but Mark wrenches away and squares off. Before anything else can happen, Jordan steps between them. "What's this all about?"

"He had me fired from my job."

John looks around the room, sees the office secretary standing before the open door, astonished, at the scene before her. He shakes his head in disbelief at what is happening.

"Tell them," Mark says.

"College," John mutters. "He doesn't want to go back."

"Well, so what?"

"He had me fired from my job. Fired a friend of mine, too."

"Mark realizes the hurt in John's eyes. He shakes his head and turns to leave, not sure now why he even came here.

Sliding behind the wheel of his car, Mark wonders what he will do now--no job, just the money from his final paycheck in his pocket, and the couple hundred he has in the bank--wonders where he will go now that he no longer has a home.

He drives slowly through the neighborhood that is as close to poverty as can be found in Oakridge. A few houses stand out from the others, those that have been cared for through the years, getting painted when they need it, repaired, roofed, and so on. An old man sits before a small cement block house with flowers planted in rows along its front, sits rocking slowly in the sun. Mark watches him, wishes for a moment that he could be him.

The old man waves a greeting to Mark. Surprised, Mark waves back. He pictures himself at college, on one of the many walkways that crisscross the campus. He is by himself on the way to class, and a girl is walking toward him. He watches her, looks for her eyes, some signal that she has seen him, that they might recognize one another's existence with a nod or "hello." But as he nears her and again looks for her eyes, he sees that she is looking straight ahead, not at him, and he watches out of the corner of his eyes for her eyes to look for his, and then she is gone and Mark walks onward, passes more solitary walkers, and feels uncomfortable that none of them seek his eyes or speak. Occasionally, one of them will meet Mark's gaze and then, as much out of embarrassment as anything else, the two will exchange meek hellos.

But the old man, Mark thinks, sits there and waves at people, strangers to him, sits and waves and smiles and rocks away his time. How can that old man have it together so well?

Mark drives past the picket line at the carton company. He is not one of them, has no claim to a job here; but he also knows he is not one of those on the other side. But then, he asks himself, where does he fit in?

He thinks of school again. He, like Amy, was supposed to be back today. His fraternity is having hell week, and as the thoughts of pouring syrup in people's hair, throwing flour on them, making the pledges push eggs around the basement floor with their noses, eat weird things, enter his mind, he wonders at his own hell week the fall before, when he had gone through the ridiculous rites, wonders how he could have degraded himself all for the sake of a few social advantages. And now he realizes that he doesn't have one real friend at the fraternity, not one he feels as close to as he does to Frank. He has just plodded along so far in his life, letting his parents tell him what he wants to be, what he should join, and what the probable results would be from taking certain actions and following certain courses. Confused, Mark parks behind the Grotto.

John sits at his desk thinking and wondering about Mark: his hatred, his apparently lost sense of values. John remembers his own college experience, how he had to work and scrimp and save, barely managing to stay caught up in his studies, juggling his school work and his evening job as a busboy at the restaurant. How he would have celebrated had anyone offered to pay for just one semester of his schooling. He thinks of that time of struggle. Jean came along and his life was better, the drudgery seemingly removed.

But none of that matters, John tells himself as he looks around his office, focusing on the present. Something is going wrong with what he and Jean have taken for granted for so many years. And Mark. He remembers how he would check the sleeping baby, watch in the dim glow of the nightlight for the tiny, quick breaths, finally see the hand-size chest move, listen intently for the whispers of life coming from the tiny, blanketed body of his son. If only Mark would see.

Tiredly John packs his briefcase with the work he will do at home this evening. Jean will be with him. Things are good more than bad, and he needs her now— to talk, to share his sorrow, to know that she loves him.

His heavy briefcase hanging at his side, he wonders what Mark is doing, wonders if he will come back home after what has happened. John wants him to come back in spite of his shame at what happened here at the office this afternoon.

He takes a deep breath and steps into the foyer of his office. The secretary is coming through the doorway of Jordan's room carrying a pile of folders. "Have a good evening, Mr. Holz," she calls to him.

"You too," he answers, and steps into the hallway to run the gauntlet of staring curiosity that he knows will accompany him. He looks ahead and walks quickly, speaking to no one until the receptionist bids him good night.

Chapter 9

The bar is packed, the wildcatters gathered to discuss strategy and celebrate the temporary shutdown. The jukebox blares while the dancing girl is gyrating, bouncing, rubbing herself on the pole before her. Then she'll turn and watch herself in the mirror, making sure that she is looking good, that her rhythm is right.

"What's happening?" Frank asks as he takes the stool next to Mark.

"Not much, man," Mark says and turns to face Frank.

"Couple more beers here," Frank says to the bartender as he walks by carrying a pitcher. "You don't look too happy."

"Don't you know why we got fired?"

"Been thinking on it, but I've been busy drinking. Hard to do both." Frank laughs and draws a laugh from Mark, but Mark loses the humor quickly.

"My old man had us fired. Fired me so I'd have to go back to school; fired you, I guess, just on general principles, maybe to show how much power he thinks he has or something."

"Damn. Your old man plays rough."

"Yeah. I think I paid him back though. Messed his day up." Mark explains the turn of events, and Frank is roaring his deep laugh by the end of the story. Mark can't help joining him.

"Couple of shots of Kessler's here," Frank shouts down to the bartender.

"How come we, you, you're always laughing?" Mark asks, the question popping out of its own accord.

Frank laughs at the question. "Don't know for sure. If you look at things from the right direction, you can get a laugh out of just about anything. My old man laughed all the time. Guess maybe that's where a good part of it comes from. Hell, he had more to cry about than laugh about, but he just saw it'd be a lot easier on everybody if he laughed."

"Cheers," Mark says and downs the shot.

"Let's get something to eat," Frank suggests shortly, and they wade through the crowd.

Freddie's bar, in an old neighborhood on the main route, serves dinners. When they are seated in one of the old high-backed, wooden booths, sipping on another beer and waiting for their food, Frank drops a couple hearts on the table before Mark. "If we're going to get ripped, might as well do it right."

Mark laughs, putting the earlier part of the day behind him, and washes the little pills down. By the time they have finished eating, Mark can already feel the speed lifting him off, feel the power of mind and body as the amphetamine pushes through the alcohol. They head out, planning to go back to the Grotto, but find themselves on Reed Road and stop to see Max.

Several children are playing in the huge yard to the side of the house, the biggest child, who looks to be about ten, pointing to something and explaining, evidently in charge. They find Max in the kitchen, cleaning up the supper dishes. "Hey, good to see you," he calls to Mark and Frank as they come through the room where the band played a couple days earlier. "Thought you were the kids when I heard you come in. Getting ready to chase you back outside," he says as he wipes his hands on a dish towel.

"Can't stay long," Frank says. "Just in the neighborhood and thought we'd stop by."

"At least have a beer with me," Max says, anxious for their company. Mark and Frank stand in the kitchen sipping their drinks while Max finishes the dishes. "Heard from Susan the other day," he volunteers.

"Where's she at?" Frank asks.

Mark is quiet, letting the strength roll over him in waves, and he watches and listens. All he knows about Max's wife is what Frank told him early in the summer: she left him and was in California living with some other guy.

Max pulls his hand out of the suds and takes a swig. "Same place. Asked me not to file for divorce yet. I'm not filing. The kids need their mother. I think she'll be back pretty soon," he says and dunks a greasy frying pan into the water.

"She'll be back." Max nods hopefully.

In a couple of minutes they are seated on the big front porch, shaded now as the sun has made its way toward the horizon, and a breeze is beginning to break up the stagnant heat. Frank lights a joint and passes it to Max.

"Good stuff," Max comments, and hands it to Mark.

"Same as you got," Frank laughs. "You ought to know it's good." Soon they are rapping away as they are enveloped by the fuzzy grass cloud. Mark, hitting his high with the speed and grass, explains all about the strike at the carton company, explains his whole day, the office at the metal works, the hearts, tells how he has come to be where he is at the present moment, that he has to be where he is or he wouldn't be himself. Frank and Max are laughing as Mark finishes his rushing rap, and he settles back, satisfied for the moment with things as they are.

He sinks back into the seemingly endless corridors of his mind, losing track of what is happening, just feeling the soothing power of the stuff he has eaten, drunk, smoked.

They sit on the porch, silent for the most part, sipping on a second beer as the evening turns to dusk, and then Max is rounding up the kids and giving the older boy instructions about baths, telling him where the clean sheets are so one of them can be making up his bed while the other one bathes.

Soon Mark and Frank are on their way again. They start for the Grotto, but when they reach Pete's Place stop there for a quick one. Inside, the light is dim except for the yellow glare of bare bulbs at either end of the shuffleboard game against the far wall. "Play you for a beer," Frank says.

"Sure."

Frank orders shots and beers. "Give the Indian over there a round too," Frank says as he notices the stranger with long, black hair hanging in strings over his shoulders, capped by a broad-brimmed felt hat. The Indian raises his glass as a thank you when the bartender sets a boilermaker before him.

Mark stands sighting down the long, wooden runway and lets loose with his first shot. They've played two games, splitting one apiece, when Frank calls over to the Indian to join them. He doesn't answer, but in a couple of minutes is standing behind them, watching the game. "Here, take over," Frank says and heads for the john at the back of the room. The Indian takes aim and shoves his steel puck hard into the wall at the end of the alley.

"Slippery," he says to himself as he steps back.

They play three more games, letting the Indian play two of them. Then Mark and Frank are ready to leave, once again planning to go back to the Grotto to finish out their evening. "Where you from?" Frank asks their silent friend.

He holds out his thumb to indicate he is hitchhiking.

"Come on, we'll give you a lift to the city limits. They got some kind of law against hitchhiking in town here." The Indian nods and follows them outside.

"Which way you headed?" Mark asks.

"North."

Mark drives through town on the main route, but before they have gone far the Indian asks, "Where you guys going?"

"Going to outer space, old buddy, going to get stinking drunk and tear a new asshole for the fine city of Oakridge."

"Need any help?"

"Need all the help we can get. But now, you got to know what you're getting yourself into. We ain't drunk until we're passed out or knocked out."

"I need to get drunk," the Indian says seriously.

The Grotto is all noise and smoke and jukebox music and talking. The go-go girl, a different one now, is bumping and grinding and swiveling away up front where a cluster of customers stand watching. There are catcalls, laughter, a brief push-and-shove fight along the bar where the other dancer sits in her skimpy outfit.

"Hey, Frank," someone calls, and Mark and the Indian follow Frank to a booth at the end of the bar. Someone hands Mark a joint. When he reaches the table, Frank and the Indian are seated, Frank already engrossed in conversation with a co-worker, the Indian straining to see the go-go girl through the crowd. Mark is starting to feel the alcohol again, the speed having done double duty and now wearing thin.

They sit for a couple hours, not talking much because of the noise in the place, drinking boilermakers. Then there is an uproar of cheers and clapping, and they look to see that one of the dancers is on top of the long bar. Someone reaches up and pulls her panties to the side and sticks a dollar bill inside. She laughs and does her bump and grind above the guy, and the cheers and catcalls are there again, and she is moving down the bar, more dollar bills sticking out from the elastic crotch of her pants, and then her panties are down around her ankles, dollar bills dropping all over the bar top, but she pays the money no attention, steps out of her pants and continues her dancing, thoroughly enjoying her role. The Indian has walked over to the bar and stands at the only free spot, down at the end, waiting, watching. And finally she reaches him, and he is ready, looking up, and the Indian lunges, getting a lick, the dancer bumping and grinding, and then he is gone, having fallen over in his drunkenness. He sits against the end of the bar, smiling a silly grin. The theatre of the absurd is over, though, the owner of the bar leading the dancer back to the rest room where she can dress, a few boos coming from the crowd as the dance ends.

The Indian makes it back to the table, and they have one more round before the one o'clock closing. Then it's time to go, and Mark stands up unsteadily, so drunk and crazy by now that he is not even aware he's drunk. Frank helps the Indian out to the car, where he crawls into the back seat and passes out. There is nothing to be said now; Mark and Frank are numb and ready to fall into bed somewhere and pass out along with the Indian.

But the turbulent emotions of earlier in the day seep through Mark's drunkenness, come into focus, looming consumingly over him, and he is angry all over again, angry at his father, at Oakridge, angry at anything and everything. He punches the accelerator to the floor and speeds through a residential neighborhood, the old V-8 whining as it winds out, and he is doing seventy through a stop sign, and then realizes what he is doing and pulls the shifter into low gear. Mark finds himself in front of the grade school he attended as a child. And the anger is there again as he pictures himself taunting the bald, retarded boy of fourteen in his second grade class, throwing snowballs at the poor guy on the playground at recess, hates himself for the meanness and mindlessness of childhood, sees his fifth grade teacher, never smiling, hating her job and the kids that went along with it, pictures her cracking his hands with the edge of the ruler, sees her ugly and angry face, pictures himself in the role of a pine cone in the fourth grade Christmas pageant and damn the place, damn the people who all helped make it happen, damn the building itself.

He swerves the car onto the grass in front of the school, tearing ruts out of the yard with his rear wheels, turf and dirt flying as the car spins in a circle, and then before him is a skinny tree, and he floors the accelerator, the wheels spinning faster in the yard, faster and faster until the tree is near, and then he is thrown into the steering wheel as the car collides with the tree, the Indian falls off the back seat and onto the floor, and Frank is yelling, "You trying to kill us?"

Mark falls out of the car, sees the front fender buckled out at least a foot and stands there kicking it, falling down, getting back up and kicking and falling. Then Frank is there, dragging him around to the passenger side of the car as a light comes on across the street. Frank jumps behind the wheel and backs away from the tree, and the Indian is sitting up in the back seat saying what the fuck's happening, and the wheels are spinning for traction as Frank guns the engine.

"Damn the place," Mark keeps saying, but finally Frank makes him realize what has happened, that there are going to be cops looking for them and the car, that they've got to get wherever they're going quickly.

The Indian passes out again, and in a couple of minutes they are at Frank's apartment, Frank telling Mark to get home and hide the car, and Mark sees, yes, he must get home and into his house into bed, and somehow he makes it there, makes it out of his car and into the house where he falls down, and then he is in his room, face first on his bed, passed out, his rage gone now   in   this   blind   numbness.

Chapter 10

The knock is steady pounding as John gets up and pulls on his robe, muttering to himself in his half-sleep. One of the cops holds a flashlight on his face when he opens the door, and he puts his hand up to shield his eyes.

"Oakridge Police," the flashlight bearer says stiffly.

"I don't give a damn who you are. Get that light out of my eyes."

"Yessir. Is this the residence of Mark Holz?"

John is thrust wide awake. "Has something happened to him?"

"We're trying to find out now what happened tonight. That is his car in the driveway?"

John steps out the door to where he can see Mark's old Chevy. There is another cop by the car with a flashlight, kneeling down to look at the sod caked under the rear fenders.

Jean's voice comes from the kitchen. "What is it, John?"

He ignores her and stands looking at the car. "How come the lights are on?" John asks as he sees the weak beams shining against the garage.

"That's the way we found the vehicle. It fits the description of the car seen at an accident. We were just going by on patrol when we saw it," the cop explains, evidently intrigued by his role in this mystery.

The other cop joins them. "That's the car. Now all we need is the driver."

John calls in to Jean, who is waiting inside, "See if

Mark's here." The door on the far side of the car bursts open, and a dark figure lurches into the woods along the driveway. John and the cops see only the outline of the Indian. The cop who has been inspecting the car yells, "Halt! Police!" But the Indian has a good start, and he's not about to stop for anybody. The cop yells, "Halt!" again and fires his service revolver into the air.

"What the hell's the matter with you?" John says to him.

"Suspect running from the car. How do we know the car wasn't stolen?"

John pounces on the blunder. "That's it, exactly. The car was stolen and in an accident."

The cops stand silently. Flood lights are coming on in the big homes around the Holz's. But the cop who fired the shot still sees his way clear to an arrest. "How do you suppose the car ended up at it's owner's address if it was stolen?"

"Thieves aren't too smart sometimes."

"He's in bed, but I can't wake him," Jean calls.

John plunges into the house, one of the cops right behind him. John hears him and stops at the hallway to the bedrooms. "Where do you think you're going?"

"To see the suspect."

"You're going to be a suspect in a minute if you don't get out of here."

The cop backs off and retreats to the door. "You may be harboring a fugitive from the law," he warns.

"You'll get your fugitive after I've talked to my lawyer," John says. "Now get out of here."

John shakes Mark, who groans and drops back onto his face. "Drunk as hell. See if you can wake him up," John says and heads into the kitchen to call his lawyer.

Jean sits down on the bed. "Mark," she says softly. "You've got to wake up. Honey," she says and lays her head against his.

He has heard the voices again and seen the horse on the cobblestones. Now he is lying on the floor of the green room, someone calling his name. It is a wonderful, heavenly voice, and he sees the beautiful, dark-haired girl who has come into the room to help him, and her touch is soft and comforting. He is sick, knows as he is lying on the floor of the green room that he is dying, that the beautiful voice is a farewell from life.

One of the cops is back in the house, and John tells him they can arrest Mark, as the lawyer advised. John leads him to the bedroom where he finds that Jean has not been able to rouse Mark.

Mark rolls over, groaning as the room surrounds him, as the draft from an open stairwell swirls past him. What is he doing in this place? How can he get out?

There is a skylight to the green room, Mark realizes. And it's a powerful light, soft and beautiful as it floods down upon his sick and dying figure.

The cop puts his flashlight back on his belt. "Just drunk," he says and pokes Mark a couple times in the ribs with his hickory club.

And the death is final now, the morgue workers rough in their handling of his body. But he cannot understand why he can still be conscious in death.

Then he sits upright, sits in confusion as the next few moments bring him back to Oakridge from his death in the green room somewhere in Europe.

"Come peaceable now," the cop warns, still holding his stick.

Mark sits on the edge of the bed, trying to figure out

where he is, crazy as he's ever been in his life. He jumps up, feeling the anger of the day return to him, and punches a hole in the wall paneling. The other cop comes running through the house when he hears the thump, carrying *his* nightstick. The cop in the bedroom has backed away, waiting to see if Mark is going to try to hit him. "Little belligerent?"

John Holz steps between Mark, who is leaning dizzily against the wall, and the cops. John pokes a finger into the first cop's chest. "If there's any clubbing to be done in this house I'll be in on it. If you two can't get a boy to the police station without beating him up, you better call out the whole force, because you'll need it to get past me."

"Yes, where do you think you are, on television?" Jean asks and stands beside John.

"Standard procedure with belligerent suspects," the second cop mumbles as the two put their sticks back in their belt holders.

"I'm all right," Mark says, and walks between them. He already has the cruiser door open and is getting in the front seat when they reach him.

"Back seat there, buddy," one of the cops says. Mark sits behind the wire cage that separates him from the officers, and they lock him in.

Then they are at the police station, taking Mark's fingerprints, asking him questions about the wreck, taking everything out of his pockets and laying the articles out on the desk. "The belt, take it off," one of the cops says.

Mark laughs, can't help himself: something to laugh about. "You think I'm going to hang myself?"

"Don't get smart."

Then John Holz is there in the outer office discussing the bail with the desk officer. When they are done with Mark and have charged him with drunken driving, reckless operation and leaving the scene of an accident, John stands at the desk counting out the five hundred dollar bond. But Mark tells him he isn't going home with him.

"What are you talking about?" John stands in bewilderment as Mark asks the cop which way to the cells, and starts off the way he points. He is led up a cold, damp stairway to a cement and steel room with a bare light bulb hanging from the ceiling. They put him in a cell with another man, a very small man, it seems to Mark, as he lays on the bare mattress watching his cellmate before passing out again.

Mark wakes in the morning to find his companion sitting across the way on the other bunk, staring at him. "Man, you really tied one on."

"Or it tied me on," Mark says, sitting up, feeling the headache and the shakes coming on strong. He looks around the cell, with its two bare mattress bunks and the toilet and sink midway between them. "This place is a real bummer."

"No shit."

Mark looks at his companion then, something familiar about the skinny, colorless little man. "What you in here for?"

"Stole a car battery."

"You just in for the night?"

"Been here for ten days so far."

"What?" Mark asks in disbelief. "For a car battery?"

"I don't have no money to pay the fine. They won't take it out of the welfare money. Said it's for the kids.

But see," the other says intently, "I had this job lined up, see? And I needed the battery for my car so I could get to the job. But they wouldn't let me out for the job." The two are silent for a couple of minutes, then the little guy asks Mark what he's in for.

"They'll hang you for those charges. Hey, counterfeiter," he calls to somebody down the way. "Got a drunk driver over here."

The counterfeiter laughs but doesn't answer. "Got him in here on a drunk drivin' charge," he says, motioning to the next cell, "and found a roll of fake money in his pocket."

"Yeah. That was in the paper, wasn't it?"

"Yeah. He's going to the big house when they're through with him here. You don't remember me, do you?"

"I keep thinking I ought to know you from somewhere, but I can't place it. From high school, maybe?"

"Nah, I quit soon's I got to ninth grade. You used to have a paper route."

"Yeah," Mark says, picturing the ink-stained booths in the pressroom where they lined up and counted out their papers. "Yeah, now I remember. You had a booth right behind me."

"Yeah," the other says and smiles at this remembrance of a time when he had all the money he needed—for pop, and cigarettes and candy. "You had a Schwinn bicycle with gears and everything," he says to Mark.

"Yeah, right. Those were good times."

After a while Mark is feeling really bad. "What time's breakfast?" he asks.

"You slept through it. Don't know as I'd call it breakfast anyway. Toast and black coffee."

Mark sits for a few minutes, then asks how he gets through to the cops downstairs. The other laughs. "If you make enough noise they'll usually come up."

Mark shouts a couple times, his voice echoing back from the top of the stairwell. "Have to beat on the bars, so they think maybe you're goin' to bust something."

Mark kicks against the door and feels the cement floor vibrate, and the play in the door lets it make a satisfying, clanging noise. He kicks at the door until a cop comes into the room.

"Who the hell's making all the racket?"

"I want out of here."

"You're Holz. Yeah. You're going to court in a few minutes. No sense you getting out now."

In fifteen minutes another cop comes and opens the cell door. "Follow me," he orders Mark. Downstairs they enter a little room, and Mark sits where the cop points. The officer who arrested him last night is sitting beside the mayor. Beside Mark sits Gene Cowley, his father's lawyer. He leans close to Mark and whispers, "Just keep quiet. Let me do the talking."

In a short time the lawyer has backed the mayor into a corner and made his final offer: reduce the charges to reckless operation, or have a jury trial which the city can't win.

The mayor acts important and serious, knowing he really has no choice in the matter. "I'll go along with that, provided that we levy the maximum fine for the charge."

"That's reasonable," the lawyer says, and the judge pronounces Mark guilty of reckless operation, with a

$250 dollar fine.

Mark walks slowly from the room behind the lawyer. "That wasn't so bad, was it?" Cowley turns and says. "But you're lucky. Come on, your dad asked me to run you home when we were finished."

Mark follows him meekly through the lobby of the city building and out to the new Mark V, and in a few minutes they are at the Holz residence. Mark sees his father's Oldsmobile parked by the side door of the house, and as he walks closer sees that the car is packed with his clothes and other belongings.

John meets him at the door and waves to Gene as the lawyer backs out of the driveway. "Get in," he says to Mark.

Mark does as he is told, gets in the front seat of the big car and stares ahead at his battered Chevy where it sits from the night before. As they back out, Mark sees his mother, still dressed in her bathrobe, standing in the driveway waving good-bye, and Mark waves back, finally,   he   guesses,   off   to   college.

Chapter 11

The rest of the week passes, and John and Jean hear nothing from Mark. Apparently, as they had hoped, getting him back to his friends at college and exposing him to the many activities of the campus and fraternity have solved the problem of getting him on the right path.

John has been especially busy with his job, planning for the presentation he will give in Columbus on Friday at a conference and show of heavy equipment manufacturers. He has helped Blatt Metal get a good volume of work in the past in this area of industry, selling sprockets, wheels, pulley systems, plus a variety of gear boxes, and is confident that he can come from the show with several big orders even though the recent recession has drastically reduced his sales.

Jean has spent the week in quiet anticipation of her return to college, working on her story for several hours, thinking how she wants it to be and thinking about the things she would like to make happen in her life during the next year or two.

The next morning Jean is up at six, unable to sleep longer. Her first class doesn't start until eleven, but here she is, the sun not up far enough to begin burning the dew off the lawn, and she is too excited to sleep. She has drunk two cups of coffee when a thought, devastating in its importance to her, strikes: What will she wear?

By the time John is up she has worked herself into a

state of agitation over the troubling question. It is all she can do to get John's breakfast, and even then she forgets to make the toast.

John notices her excitement this morning and kids her about it, but she takes little notice of him. When he has finally left, she scans the right side of the closet, her dressy side. Then she is looking through the other side, her casual clothes, looking through the double knit pant suits and skirts.

Finally she chooses the plaid skirt she bought last week, matches it with the rust-colored silk blouse John gave her for her birthday, and applies her usual dose of makeup.

At 10:30 she is there, driving through the huge parking lot looking for a space close to the nearest building. Finally she finds a spot and gets out, checking at the same time to see that she has a pen in her purse and that her newly purchased notebook is there also. Everything together, she takes off across the parking lot, walking quickly, setting her sights on the closest building and hoping it is the right one.

So far Mark hasn't bought any of his textbooks, and instead of opening a checking account with the three hundred dollars John gave him to get started, Mark carries the wad of bills in his billfold. He has already spent a hundred of it—forty dollars for a bag of dope and the rest on beer and food. He knows that at this rate he will soon be broke, especially if he buys the books that his professors have required. Then, he knows, it will be back to John for more money, explaining how he went through three hundred smackers in record time.

And he has no desire to explain anything to him at this point. Yet he knows that he is totally dependent upon him for his food, clothing, and shelter.

By Friday he has gone to only half his classes and is so lethargic that he cannot even get out of bed. When he does get up at noon there is a letter for him.

Dear Mark,

Dad told me that you decided to go back to school. I'm so glad you did. I know how you felt about it but you're doing the best thing. My first year here at school I wanted to quit. But I decided to make it to Thanksgiving. And once I made it that far and got back home for a few days, all I had to do was make it to Christmas, which was easy. Anyways what I'm trying to say is take a little bit at a time, and besides, what else is there that you could be doing?

Keeping busy with everything at the sorority— choosing a new pledge class and all— and carrying a pretty good load this quarter. Write to me when you can. Or better, come down some weekend.

Love,
Amy

He rereads it and lets his imagination conjure Amy for him. He's glad she signed it "Love."

The day at the power systems show has been a huge disappointment for John. He has demonstrated, explained, and talked up the superior products available from Blatt Metal Works. But the purchasing agents for the major companies—Caterpillar, Deere, International, Dresser Industries—have been wary, acting, John thinks, as though he is trying to sell them something that is no longer needed.

Blatt Metal's exhibition booth is cheap and incomplete compared to the stiff competition John finds this year. Two Japanese firms have elaborate demonstrations of their products, twice the floor space that John rented for the show, and constant movie clips showing their modern manufacturing facilities, the many applications of their products, and the companies that use their equipment.

The day over, John is packing up his few belongings and giving the hourly worker from the plant his orders. Maybe, if Jordan hadn't been around, John could have gotten a little of the business that the Japanese firms so easily swallowed up. After the rep from the farm equipment company told John that his company would be canceling their orders for gear boxes the first of the year, Jordan got all excited and jumped into the conversation that John wanted to handle, asking the rep why he would buy foreign goods, citing the trade deficit and other political clichés. John would have liked to get the rep in the bar across the street, buy him a couple of drinks and discuss the situation, ask for a stay of execution for one of his biggest accounts, lie to him, flatter him, whatever it would take.

John thinks of the lack of orders from the show as he packs his briefcase, the dismal failure at the place where he can usually make a few easy thousand every fall, thinks of the pulley system Blatt Metal had sold so successfully in the past to a crane manufacturer which is now going to start making its own system more cheaply than John can sell it. For his day's work John comes away with a parts order for gears and pulleys and an order for a small die. And John is not even sure that Blatt's engineer can come up with a design for the die. It's worth a try at least, John is thinking, and he'll get a good commission on such a specialized and expensive job.

John is on his way out of the show building when Don Weston, a salesman for a stamping company in Portsmouth, hails him from across the aisle. They have been friends for years.

"Do any good?" Weston asks. "Been meaning to get over to talk to you all day, but I've been busier than hell. Went into plastic extrusion this year, you know."

"Didn't do well at all," John says as he grasps Don's hand.

"Sorry to hear that. This plastic extrusion thing is really catching on. Got an order from Ford, believe it or not, to make parts for the bumper system. If I can just get engineering and production to go on this, we can double our extrusion line in a year."

"That's good to hear," John says, sincere in his wishes of success for Don. "That's part of our problem, not doing anything new, not taking any chances."

"Let me buy you a drink," Don says. "I'm out of here in five minutes."

John starts to say no, thinks for a moment of his doctor's orders not to drink, thinks of his ulcer still throbbing away, and says to hell with it, a drink is exactly what he needs.

In ten minutes the two are sitting in the plush lounge

of the Holiday Inn. Don is talking animatedly about the expansion of his plant, the bright outlook for the next several years, his son in medical school, his daughter who is finishing her MBA at Ohio State, and his wife who was elected to city council last year.

John drinks, has his vodka and tonic put away before Don is halfway through, and orders them another round. John has been silent, nodding and nurturing Don's monologue, but after the second drink he is calmed somewhat. As Don has asked about his family, John tells about Mark, who is doing well in school—planning to go to law school. And John is able to air his complaints about the Japanese firms which did a job on him and Blatt Metal, borrowing Jordan's ill-timed clichés about foreign businesses, their cheap labor, and the government's sanction of letting them dump cheap goods on the market.

An hour later, after a couple more drinks, John and Weston shake hands in the parking lot, promising to look each other up when they're near each other's homes. Don mentions that they are looking for a manufacturer's rep to cover Indiana and Illinois for the company, and John says, sure, he'll think about it, maybe a change would be good and there's money to be made selling independently.

And then he is on his way, the air conditioning feeling good as he guides his new Olds up Interstate 71. He sets the cruise control on 55, turns up the FM stereo volume and settles back for the drive. The failure at the show and his lack of orders from it are temporarily blotted out, and he feels good, thinks ahead to tomorrow and the first round of the county golf tournament. He was runner-up last year in the championship flight and he thinks now that he can win it this year if he gets his game under control in the first round. He pictures himself holding the two foot trophy. And the vision makes him feel good, smoothes out some of the turbulent things that have been happening to him lately.

The car has a wheel out of balance, and he frets for a while over trying to determine which wheel is causing the vibration. When he finally gets off the freeway and heads toward Cranston, he is beginning to feel irritable: The liquor is wearing off, and he finds himself once again dwelling on unpleasant things. He thinks about how he had to lie to Don about Mark's schooling; he thinks about the Japanese imports taking away one of his biggest accounts, and by the time he has fought his way through the rush hour traffic in Cranston and is on the last leg of his trip to Oakridge, he is agitated again, his ulcer sizzling away, and wants only to get home where he can hide and have another drink.

In the distance John sees a bicycle rider on the highway, and as he approaches, sees another car come around the hilly curve about a quarter mile away. He has to slow down as he sees that the car is going to pass the bicycle at the same time he is, and has nearly stopped when the cyclist turns off the highway onto a county road. The other car passes, and John starts to pick up speed, trying again to figure which wheel is out of balance, when a long blast from a car's horn startles him. He glances in the rearview mirror and sees a lopsided, rusty-green Plymouth closing on him. Then the old, green car is in the other lane spewing black smoke from its exhaust as the driver pushes to pass.

John is enraged, the day's problems, the things that have been happening for weeks combining with the alcohol edginess to throw him into a fury. He floors the accelerator, and the big V-8 whines into passing gear, quickly pulling John even with the Plymouth.

Then a pickup truck in the other lane comes into John's view as he starts around the curve. He slams on his brakes, knows there is going to be an accident, knows that there is no way around it, but it is too late for the driver of the green car to adjust. The rocky hillside obscures the pickup from the driver until it is too late, and as John's Olds goes into a slide, the pickup plows head-on into the other car.

Then all is noise as the two vehicles explode into each other, breaking glass and pieces of steel peeling off and filling the air. The pickup glances off the Plymouth and swings around, tires squealing, standing on two wheels for a moment, and then bounces off the side of John's car, finally coming to a rest upside down. The old Plymouth, what is left of it, plows into the rock wall on the curve.

John's Olds finally comes to a stop, and he sits dumbly behind the wheel staring at a piece of green quarter panel that has come to rest on the hood of his car. Then he is trying to open his door, but it's jammed tight from the collision with the truck, and he butts it repeatedly with his shoulder until it pops open.

What to do? He stands behind his car, knows nothing else in the world except that there is a pickup truck lying upside down fifty yards away, its wheels spinning crazily, and a green car, smashed in as if it were a tin can, lying at the base of the rocky hillside, and people dead or dying. John starts running toward the pickup. Halfway there he sees a man crawling out the window.

As John reaches the man, a car comes slowly upon

the scene, and he shouts, "Get ambulances! Get an ambulance!" The other car speeds away, leaving John with the bloody figure.

He looks inside the truck to see if there are any more passengers, and then kneels beside the man, who is moaning in pain, his face bloody, and John pulls him from the roadway to the grassy ditch along the road.

John kneels beside him again, sees that he is breathing well even though he looks a mess, and then is up and running toward the green car. He runs, faster than he has moved for years, and in a few moments is standing next to the squashed car, breathing hard. Then he sees the blood along the crumpled, sun faded dashboard, walks around the other side and sees the body squashed into the seat by the steering wheel, sees the head tilted at a crazy angle and the arm sticking grotesquely through the spokes of the steering wheel.

John walks to the ditch, where he kneels and retches into the long grass.

He hears a siren, and finally the ambulance arrives. He motions frantically from the ditch beside the pickup. The emergency van comes to a stop and two men jump out. They pull the stretcher from the van and lay it beside the man in the ditch. John has spent the last ten minutes tending to the man, talking to him, assuring him that he is going to be all right, and now John stands dumbly as the attendants determine what is broken and what is not.

John wanders a few yards away as he hears more sirens, and a state patrol car comes into view. One of the attendants orders him, "Support his back."

John stares blankly. "Come here!" comes the order. "Hold your hands beneath his back." Only when he is helping them does John see the bone protruding from the thigh, and once again he feels the phlegm rise and squirt sourly into the back of his mouth. Then they have the man on the stretcher and quickly stow it in the van, one of them in the back now, fixing a hypo to ease the pain. The patrol car roars up to them.

Quickly the trooper estimates the situation. "Anyone injured in the truck? You," he shouts at John. "Anyone in the truck?"

"No," John says as the van squeals away. Another ambulance is stopping by the green car, and behind it is another patrol car. John walks slowly toward the activity around the old Plymouth and watches as the patrolman sets to work with the ambulance attendants, using a crowbar, trying to force open the car door. John starts across the highway, thinking he can help, but retreats to his car, realizing that there is nothing to be done. He leans against the crumpled fender, cups his throbbing forehead in the palm of his hand and waits.

In ten minutes they have extracted the mangled body from the car. A county sheriff's cruiser has arrived also, and the two additional officers take over clearing the debris from the roadway. Soon they take over traffic control from the state police. Then one of the patrolmen is measuring the distance between the vehicles with a little wheel on a stick and taking pictures of everything in sight.

John stands numbly, still leaning against his car, as the other patrolman approaches. "Can you tell us what happened?" he asks John. The cop pulls a notebook and pen out of his back pocket. "Are you okay?" he asks when he receives no answer.

"Yeah, I'm all right. It just happened so fast. He's

dead, isn't he?"

"Yeah. This is your car?" the trooper says, motioning to the Olds.

"Yes."

"Are you able to tell me how it happened?"

John doesn't answer, and the cop lays his notebook on the sprung trunk lid. "Come over here and lie down." When John is lying on the grass along the berm, the cop checks his pulse, looks at the pupils of his eyes, then gets up and asks him if he wants to go to the hospital.

"No," John says.

"You're in slight shock. Not bad, but maybe you should go on into the emergency room."

John sits up then. "No. I'll be all right."

A minute later they are seated in the patrol car. "Just explain to me what you think happened," the patrolman tells him.

"It was all so fast. I was coming up on the curve and heard this horn blast behind me."

"Which way were you traveling?"

John points around the curve, and the cop scribbles the information in his notebook.

"Next thing I know this car is passing me, and then I saw the pickup coming."

"The car was traveling the same direction as you?"

"Right. I didn't know what to do except slam on my brakes. Then the pickup sideswiped me."

"Are there any witnesses? Any other cars on the scene or anything?"

"Nobody," John says, and thinks of the bicycle rider. If he saw it happen....

"Okay," the patrolman says, after looking at John's driver's license and recording his name and address.

"We may contact you later, but everything seems fairly clear. Let's go over and see whether your car is drivable."

Then the cop is giving John the okay to drive home and John is pulling slowly onto the road, taking one last look at the destruction and death.

Ten minutes later, as he is entering Oakridge, it finally hits him: he killed a man. He feels little at the moment, is only able to state the fact, but by the time he reaches home, the anxiety envelops him as he relives the details of the accident.

He parks on the concrete driveway by the Shunks' car and sits, thinking that if things had happened differently, he might be dead. At least he is alive. He tells himself that it's important he wasn't hurt, but can't really think why.

"Here he is," calls Jean as John enters the house. "Where have you been?" she asks him, a hint of agitation in her voice. "I hope the fire is still all right," she says and looks out the kitchen window to the brick barbecue in the back yard. "Why don't you go out and put some more charcoal on?" She hears no answer and turns to look at John, who has stood staring at her the whole time. "John? What's the matter?"

"Wreck," he says then. "Car accident."

"Are you all right?"

"Yeah, I'm okay. Just tired. A man was killed."

"Let's go and sit down. The Shunks are having supper with us. T-bones."

"Hey, John!" Jerry calls. "All ready for the tournament tomorrow? I've got a twenty riding on you."

"Yeah, the tournament," John says slowly.

"There was a wreck," Jean explains.

"I was in a wreck."

"You okay?"

"I think so. How about fixing me a drink, whatever everybody's having," he says, motioning to the glasses Jerry and Gertrude are holding.

"Are you sure? Your ulcer."

John waves away the idea of protecting his ulcer, and Jean quickly fixes him a bourbon and water.

"Will you check the fire?" Jean asks Jerry.

"Sure."

John sits in silence while Jerry is outside. Gertrude asks John a couple of questions, but receives no reply and joins Jean in the kitchen. Then Jerry is back, making himself another drink.

"You really got clobbered," Jerry says. "Where'd it happen?"

"That bad curve on the way to Cranston."

Jerry nods knowingly. "Been a lot of accidents there through the years. The state ought to do something to make it safer. Anybody hurt?"

"Yeah. It was bad. One dead."

"You were pretty lucky, huh?"

"I guess so."

"Let me get a paper and pen, and you can explain what happened for the newspaper tomorrow."

John takes a good slug of his drink and tells Jerry what he told the patrolman. Then Jean is back in the room telling them that everything is ready, and would John cook the steaks now? and Jerry and he go out to the backyard.

After supper Jean and Gertrude try to rekindle the good spirits that prevailed before John's arrival, but can get nothing going. John simply is not up to entering into the festivities, and after they have talked him into a game of pool in the basement rec room, which he loses to Jerry, they once again sit around the living room. Jean and Jerry and Gertrude talk about various things, but John does not join. The Shunks soon leave, Jerry wishing John good luck in the tournament tomorrow.

Jean tries to talk to John, but he wants none of it. Then she tries to snuggle up against him in the big chair, but he doesn't respond. Jean kisses him and leaves him alone.

She goes into the den, where she watches TV for a few minutes. She wants to write and has a couple of ideas fusing together. In her library, paper and pen before her, she sits working the ideas into the plot of the story and begins writing:

But before he saw them he heard a car with a loud muffler coming down the gravel road, raising a thick cloud of dust behind it as it sped onward. He laid his socket wrench on the wagon bed and watched as the car, doing at least seventy, approached the farm. Quickly then he started for the road as fast as his bad leg would let him go. His collie, he thought, and at the same moment saw the wooly-haired old fellow streak out from the shade under the front porch. Only lately the dog, in its old age, had begun chasing cars and trucks. But it only chased the ones with loud mufflers.

Jean puts her pen down and reads the story through from the beginning, making a few corrections. She glances at her watch and is dumbfounded as she sees that it is nearly midnight. Two hours passed, and she was not aware of a moment of it as one is usually aware of time, and the feeling is strangely exhilarating to her.

Then she thinks of John and hurries into the living room where she finds him asleep in his chair. She strokes his hair before she tries to wake him, watches him for a few moments and then gently shakes his shoulder. "Look out!" he says and sits up, then relaxes as he sees he is at home.

"You've got to get to bed," she says. "The golf tournament   tomorrow."

Chapter 12

Next morning, John sips a soda as he drives toward the country club, and at one point nearly decides to turn around and go back home. He killed a man yesterday, he is thinking as he drives past the state park. How can he play a game this morning?

But as he navigates the club drive and sees the parking lot filled with cars, and every hole crowded with players participating in the tournament, the excitement begins to build in him, and by the time his caddy brings his clubs to the tee John is ready, the ugly thoughts displaced by these familiar and wonderful surroundings. He gives his caddy a twenty and instructs him to buy half a dozen Titleists and some candy bars, then turns to seek out the other players who will round out his foursome. He is glad to be playing with golfers of his own ability. It gets old playing with a bunch of hackers like Blatt and Shunk, he is thinking as he shakes hands with Tony Jamison, the winner of last year's championship flight. They exchange remarks about what a good day it is for the tournament—no rain, and the humidity low with the coming of fall.

Then John is teeing the new ball, shaking from the excitement that is building. He flexes his arms to relax his shoulders, feels the whip of the driver and concentrates. And then the swing, and the ball soars perfectly down the middle of the fairway and rolls to a stop by the two hundred fifty yard marker. Then the others are off, and John is striding quickly ahead of his caddy, carrying the nine iron that he knows will be the club to use on his approach shot.

After Jean has eaten breakfast, had her coffee and straightened up the house, she starts thinking of her story again. She wonders if it is long enough as she gets her Rainbow vacuum from the hallway closet, but knows it's not important. As she vacuums the thick, gold carpet, she is thinking about what is needed to round out the story.

She leaves the vacuum cleaner and goes to her desk. She reads over her work, changing a few words here and there, adding or taking away punctuation. When she reaches the end, she has an idea and writes:

When the old man and the girls got back to the house, Grandpa took them inside and gave them each a tall glass of the Kool-aid he had bought for them. He made a special trip into town to get the stuff, had bought all his groceries the day before and when he got home had stowed away the few food-stuffs an old man needs to sustain himself, when he remembered the Kool- aid.

"Started on their way," Jean repeats to herself two hours later, repeats the last line and knows the story is finished. We're all on our way. On our way to a new life every day, on our way to our goals, on our way even without goals, on our way to death. She reads the whole story again and likes it the way it is. She has another cup of coffee, once again savoring the feeling that she has created something good, something which somehow transcends her life, something which will never die unless what we know as civilization comes to an end. And she wonders if John has ever experienced similar feelings. She'll talk to him about it, show the story to him, share these deepest feelings with him later. There are possibilities in every direction of her life. She hopes John will understand. It could open up a new realm for them, transcend their problems of late.

By midafternoon, when Jean is supposed to meet John at the country club, she has typed half of the story and finished cleaning the house, even spotting in some of the traffic marks on her vinyl kitchen floor.

At the club Jean crowds close to the scoreboard to read the names and scores, and finds that John shot a 76. Then Jerry Shunk is standing next to her. "The old man did all right," he says, grasping her arm. "He's four strokes off the lead. A kid's ahead! You know that skinny, blond-headed fellow who's always out here practicing?"

"The Henson boy?"

"Yeah. That's the one."

"Amazing."

"He was ramming in putts from all over."

"Where's John?"

"He was in the bar a while ago. Had a drink with him. He's with Jamison. He finished one stroke ahead of John. But John seems upset even though he did well. The wreck might be bothering him. It was nasty from what the state patrol told me this morning. Head-on between the two other vehicles."

"He talked about it a little last night. He thought he could have died."

"He talked about it today too."

"Maybe I can get him to come over to the pool with me," Jean says. "Get in the water and loosen up a little. Get him out of the bar and, oh, Jerry, I finished my story today."

"Good. Maybe you'll let me see it one of these days?"

"I will. As soon as I get it back from Professor Higby."

Jean finds her husband sitting at the bar by himself drinking gin.

He smiles as she sits down beside him. She orders a ginger ale. "You played well today. Are you celebrating or thinking about a couple of bad shots you made?"

"Not sure," he says, squeezing some juice from the lime in his drink. "I was hitting the ball well, all except for two holes. Double bogies. Two right in a row." John flashes the picture of his drive from the seventh hole, him standing on the tee, confident, not worried about the hazard of the woods on the left side of the fairway. And then he is taking his backswing and Hooooonk, a car behind him blares its horn from the highway as it passes another, and he can hear the whine of the V-8 again as it hits passing gear, hear the car of today and his own yesterday. And there were two strokes penalty as his ball duck-hooked into the woods. And then on the next hole, he hit his first shot in the trap, took two shots getting out and onto the green, and there it was—two double bogies and he blew his chances.

"Tomorrow you'll have a good day."

He looks to her, wondering how she knows this, and sees the excitement in her now, the energy and spark in her eyes. "Come over to the pool with me," she says.

He sits looking into his drink, poking into it with the plastic straw. "I don't feel much like swimming. Nice in here, and I have to take a shower before dinner. I'll meet you and the Shunks here at six. I have to run home.

Forgot to bring a change of clothes this morning."

Jean gone, John finishes his drink, checks the board once more, then walks over to his damaged car. He must have told the story a dozen times today; people asking, what happened to his car, and he tells them about the green car passing him on the curve and then the pickup, explaining he is lucky to be alive.

At home he finds the newspaper on the kitchen table. "SPECTACULAR CRASH KILLS AREA MAN," blares the headline. He looks through the story, reads how the old car passed him illegally and smashed into the pickup. "Clyde Johnson, the driver of the pickup, is in fair condition at Cranston General Hospital with a double fractured leg and internal injuries. Luke Baker, the driver of the other car, was killed upon impact. (See page 5 for obituary.)" John skims through the rest of the article and sees his name, the story relating that he was involved in the collision, then turns to page five.

"Area Deaths." John glances through the half dozen and picks out the name:

Luke Baker, 36, died of multiple injuries sustained in a three-car accident on Route 25 late yesterday afternoon. A recent arrival to the Oakridge area, Mr. Baker is survived by his wife, Elly, who presently resides on County Road 34, and his parents, Mr. and Mrs. Walter Baker of Matewan, W.Va. Also surviving are four brothers and one sister. In the Oakridge area Mr. Baker is survived by a nephew, Frank Baker.

He was employed by Standard Oil Co. in Cranston.

Services will be held in West Virginia. The body

was taken to the Spinley Funeral Home here. Other funeral arrangements are incomplete at this time.

John lays the paper on the table. Dear God, he sighs to himself. Frank Baker. The name jolts John from his thoughts, and he tears open the paper again. Frank Baker. He sees the gangly character standing on the diving board at the country club.

He grabs the phone book and looks up Mark's number at school. At least he can find out for sure. Then he has the number before him and dials the area code, but hangs up and sits staring dumbly at the wall. What good would it do? he asks himself after a minute. But it can't hurt to know for sure, to know if the man he killed is related to anyone he knows. For some reason he has to know, and dials the Columbus number again. Mark is soon located in the fraternity house and called to the phone.

"Mark, how are you?"

"Doing pretty good, Dad," Mark lies. "How's everything at home?"

"Good. Getting along okay in school?"

"The usual," Mark replies, lying again, having made it to only four classes the whole week.

"Thought I'd call and see how you were doing. Do you need anything?"

Mark clears his throat and tries to brush away the mental cobwebs from the joint he just shared with Pete. "Everything's so darn expensive. The textbooks alone were over a hundred dollars."

"Inflation," John says knowingly. "A couple hundred get you anywhere?"

"That would just about do it. But listen, Dad, I was

thinking of getting a job, so maybe after this you won't have to pay any more. It's about time I started earning my way."

"School's the main thing right now. Listen, I worked my way through, and it's no fun. You'll have the rest of your life to work, and that won't be any fun either. I'll mail you a check this evening."

"Thanks, Dad," Mark says, feeling ashamed for lying.

"Hey, listen, I was in a wreck yesterday."

"You okay?"

"Yeah, I'm all right, but a man was killed and another banged up bad. The one killed was Luke Baker."

"You're kidding. I knew a guy named Luke Baker. He was Frank's uncle."

John is silent, his thoughts confirmed. "That must be the one," he finally says. "Do you know anything about...how was the family fixed for money?"

"They didn't have anything. Luke was a nice sort of fellow. His wife is due to have a baby pretty soon."

"I feel bad about this, Mark. Maybe I could help them out. You see, if things had happened differently, I would be dead instead of the other fellow."

"Maybe they do need some help. They just moved up here from West Virginia, were staying at that crummy trailer park Harry Hillman runs. Frank was trying to get his uncle a better job in Oakridge."

"I'll call Frank," John says.

"Nah. He doesn't have a phone. Lives down on Pine Street though. The last house on the right before the dead end. He lives upstairs."

"Maybe I'll see him. There might be something I can do to help."

"That's good of you, Dad."

After hanging up, Mark feels rotten about how he lied to his father, and feels bad about Luke, but is glad John wants to help. He sits thinking for a while about the bright-cheeked young woman of Luke's, her stomach bulging out with a new life, and now she has nothing. He isn't in a mood to rejoin the party in his room and heads out of the fraternity house, has to get away, take a walk, clear his mind of these ugly thoughts.

Chapter 13

John makes himself a drink, then wanders into the library. He picks up Jean's manuscript. After the first four paragraphs, he lays it aside, wondering what could have possessed Jean to write such a ridiculous thing.

Suddenly John knows he has to find Frank, or Luke's wife. Right now. He has to make things right with them, get rid of the guilt that is dragging him down. He gets his checkbook, remembers the check he promised to send Mark, hurriedly makes it out and gets an envelope from the desk. As he is driving to Frank's apartment, John goes by the post office and mails the check. He feels a little better then, knowing that he is meeting his obligations to his son.

He wonders how much he should offer Luke's wife. A thousand? Two thousand? He settles on two thousand and makes a mental note to transfer a thousand from his savings account to his checking account. That will still leave five hundred in checking and should be enough until payday.

As he turns down Pine Street, an urgency replaces the agitation he felt earlier, and the urgent voice is saying, yes, get on with it, pay for this mistake and be done with it. Then he is there before the house Mark described. He ascends the rickety stairway and knocks on the door. He raps again, harder, but no one comes.

It is already after five. He hurries home, takes a quick shower and starts out to the club, still carrying his checkbook, hoping that somehow he can get this thing out of the way today, that maybe after dinner at the club he can stop again at Frank's place.

But as he approaches the club a few minutes later, he forgets about the time, remembers what Mark told him, that Luke's wife lives at Hillman's trailer camp, and the urgency is there again, pushing him on to settle this thing now, and John drives past the country club. Soon he is driving slowly back the dusty lane. Hillman brought him here once, when he was adding more trailers and wanting John to invest in it with him. But John didn't like what he saw, and turned down the offer. As far as he could figure, taking care of such a bunch of junk would have been more hassle than it was worth.

He stops at the first trailer. A child runs to the door at his knock and stands staring. "Who is it?" comes an adult voice from within. How can he say, "John Holz?" His name would mean nothing to anyone in the trailer. "I'm looking for Bakers'."

A man in a t-shirt appears at the door. "The house at the end of the lane."

John hurries back to his car. He drives past the dozen or so trailers, stops before the old farm house, then sits for a moment watching two children playing. As he steps onto the porch he catches the smell of an overloaded septic system.

He knocks on the door, fingering his checkbook in his back pocket. Then there is a young woman standing before him, silent, searching, seeming surprised to see him standing there in his expensive evening clothes.

"Is this the Baker residence?"

"Yeah, but if you're sellin' somethin', we don't want none."

"No, nothing like that. Are you Mrs. Baker?"

"No. What you want to see her about?"

Frank appears behind the woman, and recognizing John, steps onto the porch. He stands towering over John. "What do you want?"

"I'm here to…I want to, uh, you know I was involved in the accident?"

"*You* were?" Frank glances past John to the damaged car, then nods slowly as he understands. Frank stands waiting for John to explain himself, but John is at a loss for words, his thoughts telling him that he has done wrong in coming here. Won't it just cast suspicion on him that he is here, that he wants to help out in some way? And he again thinks of the bicyle rider who may have witnessed the accident. "What the hell do you want?" Frank asks, puzzled by John's appearance here, puzzled that the man who tried to have him fired from his job should come to see him.

"I want to help if I can."

"Help what?"

John pulls out his checkbook and holds it up as if to explain. But Frank says nothing, doesn't really care to understand what John wants. "I could have been the one killed instead of your uncle," John finally says.

"That would've been better."

"I think you're misunderstanding why I'm here. I talked to Mark today, and he said that maybe your aunt could use some help."

"You mean money help?"

"Yes. I'd like to help out if I can."

Frank stands looking at John, thinks of his phone correspondence with his parents and other uncles and aunts on both sides of the family, how they are all pitching in to pay to bring Luke's body down to Matewan, how they all banded together, making whatever sacrifices necessary to add their fifty or hundred dollars to the fund. Frank thinks hard, considering what John is offering, thinks again of the near loss of his job because of John, dismisses these thoughts and comes back to the starting point: accept the money or not? ''We bury our own," Frank says.

John stands in confusion. This isn't right, he tells himself; Frank is not understanding what he wants to do. "Let me give you something. With a baby coming she can use the money, surely she can."

"We take care of our own. She'll have a place to stay and family to look out for her."

John stands looking into Frank's dark, proud eyes. "Don't you understand?" John says. "I want to *give* you some money."

Frank stands before John, his arms folded across his muscular chest. "You're the one doesn't understand."

The pregnant Elly appears at the door. "What is it, Frank?"

"Finish packing," Frank tells her. "We've got to get started."

"Mrs. Baker," John calls to her, but she is already gone.

John stands there, unbelieving, trying to think of some way to make Frank see.

"Get out of here," Frank says then, and John, watching Frank unfold his powerful arms, retreats. As he approaches the club a few minutes later, he manages to smile at the outcome: he has tried to make things right—and he *did* make them right by offering the money—and now the situation is resolved and it didn't cost him a cent. How stupid Frank is, John is thinking as he parks before the shaded clubhouse. How absolutely stupid.

John is enveloped by the comfortable world of the country club, and his thoughts of Frank and Elly and Luke are gone. He finds Jean and Jerry sitting in the bar. Jean is smiling and laughs at something Jerry says. He laughs along with her, and then they are into an animated conversation on some topic or other, talking seriously, and John watches as Jerry shrugs in answer to something Jean says, and then they are laughing again. John feels the jealousy, and it hurts him somewhere deep within, hurts all over. It has been years since he and Jean could sit together so relaxed and have such a happy and carefree conversation. Gertrude approaches the table from the other end of the bar where she has been talking to Millie Blatt.

John starts through the bar. "Good game there today," Henry Trumbull calls to him from his stool.

"Thanks," John says and stops to talk for a moment. "Buy you a drink here," Henry says.

"Thanks, Henry. Wife's over here. Got to eat dinner."

Gertrude is seated with Jean and Jerry now, and John feels a little ashamed of his jealous thoughts. How would he have Jerry, his best friend, treat Jean? They sit talking, but John can't help noticing that the spark and animation between Jerry and Jean are gone now that he and Gertrude are with them.

Over their dinner, Jerry asks Jean about her writing class.

"It's the best class I've ever been in," she says. "Higby has published three novels and is really interesting to listen to. Our first story was due on Friday. I've got it done, but have to finish typing it up."

"Is that what that drivel was on your desk?" John

asks. "Why would you want to write such a thing?"

Jean turns to John, then glances at Jerry, who meets her gaze momentarily and lifts his eyebrows as if to shrug away John's slighting comment.

As the evening progresses, John finds himself once again becoming entangled in his thoughts of the accident, and the guilt descends over him. He drinks.

By midnight, when they are ready to go home, John is too drunk to drive, though he insists he is okay. Jerry is able to talk him into letting Jean drive home, pointing out that she can bring him out to the club in the morning, and then his car will be here when he is done playing.

John falls asleep on the short drive home, and Jean wakes him, struggles to help him into bed, then goes to her library to sit and look at the "drivel" she had been so proud of, wondering how John could have so ignorantly misunderstood the purpose of her returning to school, how he could be so insensitive to her ambitions. She feels a great sadness and realizes as she is retiring to bed that he must understand. Her hopes are too serious to be slighted. She deserves a chance at what she wants to do, and will not have that opportunity taken away by anyone, including her husband of twenty years.

Chapter 14

John does poorly in the tournament the next day. Jamison has a bad round, too, so John has a ready and willing drinking partner. The Henson kid shoots a seventy-one, winning all, and the older, more experienced golfers are gracious in their defeat, giving the boy so much attention and praise that by the end of the day he is certain he is going to be the next Jack Nicklaus.

Sunday night is a repeat performance at the Holz residence— John drunk again, feeling the uncontrollable mental pain that keeps pounding upon him: Killer, Murderer, come the accusations from what John can only assume is his conscience, vastly overdeveloped in childhood by his Methodist parents, but dormant for decades.

Monday, after the eleven o'clock news, Jean goes to bed by herself and lies awake as John comes to bed a few minutes later, lies there listening to him slip off his clothes in the dark, feels his weight sag the bed, and then his back is to her, and in a few moments he is asleep.

She puts on her robe, goes to the library, and takes a sleeping pill. She sits thinking about her story, which she gave to Higby today, and lets the dream of her ambitions form its random self in her mind and emotions. She reads the fiction in the latest *Atlantic,* and finally, groggy from the pill, she is able to sleep.

The next evening John comes home right after work. She is glad for this, because if he hadn't come home, she knows he would be at a bar, either at the hotel or the country club. But as he enters the house, she sees that he is in better humor. He kisses her and asks if she would like to go out for dinner.

In a half hour they are on their way to a steak house near Greenburg. They pass the evening leisurely, having cocktails before dinner, and she is glad that John is just sipping on his as she is, with no intention of getting drunk. While they are waiting for dinner, John tells her he has to be out of town for a couple of days, to make a trip to Cincinnati to service his accounts.

She takes this in stride; his job has always meant a lot of traveling, though in recent years he has had to stay on the road overnight infrequently.

Back home later, they sit and watch TV. John packs his bag for his trip and then rejoins her. They skip the evening news and go to bed. But John is impotent, a first in his life. He sits up and turns on the nightstand light. He doesn't understand it, can't see why a momentary mental picture of the wreck should so affect him, and he wants to tell Jean the truth about the accident, tell her he killed a man, but he can't tell her, can't tell anyone. One thing he is sure of: no one likes a murderer.

John is up and gone by the time Jean wakes at seven. He believes that early in the morning is the best time to catch a purchasing agent or engineer, since by afternoon most of them are working at untangling some internal problem concerning a year's supply of rubber bands or paper clips.

Jean lies on her back, relaxed and sleepy, looking at the spiral patterns of the plaster ceiling. She feels strangely calm. She wakes later with a start and jumps out of bed when she sees it is nine-thirty. When she is in the shower a few minutes later, she wonders about the feeling she experienced upon first awakening. It was odd, her falling back asleep; once she is awake in the morning, it is usually impossible for her to sleep again. But the shower feels good and she feels rested.

After social stratification class and lunch, Jean sits in Higby's class. She is early and takes her customary seat in the third row. Most of the writing students know each other now, and they greet each other and share stories and books and little personal things of their lives as they wait for class.

Higby drops his satchel on the desk, carries a thick stack of papers to the end of the first row and thumbs off several copies. As Jean looks at the paper, she is pleasantly surprised—It is her story, and she glances at the opening paragraph, then sneaks a look around the room as if expecting everyone to be looking her way. But they couldn't know who wrote it. Higby is before the class, and Jean is taken from her thoughts.

"I've already had several stories turned in, so I thought we might as well get on with the real business of our class," Higby says. "We'll read the story, then talk about it."

Several minutes pass, and whispered conversations begin to sprout from around the room. "Okay, what about it?" Higby says as he drops his copy on the desk.

"I think it's really well written," a girl on the far side of the room says. A couple of others nod and murmur agreement.

Then David, so serious Jean thinks he is either a genius or insane, joins the conversation. "It seems to be done well enough, but it's got no guts. Little girls, Grandpa, dead doggy, new puppy. It's too sentimental and tries to pack too much meaning."

There is a silence as they wait for the boy to continue, but in a few moments he is doodling on his notebook. Jean has a strong urge to defend her story, feels a strong dislike for the boy, but manages to remain silent. Besides, she doesn't want anyone to know she wrote the thing if no one defends it from his harsh critique.

But Mrs.Welt comes to the rescue, defending against all David criticized.

David doesn't look up. "How about that?" Higby asks him. "Do you still think the story is sentimental and poorly developed?"

"I guess it just doesn't do anything for me," he says and resumes doodling.

Others offer suggestions for improving the story, or praise it, liking it the way it is; and very soon, it seems to Jean, the class is over, and she is on her way out with the others. Higby meets her at the doorway. "Coffee?"

Jean thinks ahead to the afternoon. She has no committments. "Sure," she says, and they descend the stairway to the cafeteria and get their drinks.

"You didn't have much to say about the story."

"I usually try to stay out of the way if the discussion brings out everything that needs to be talked about."

He takes a copy out of his satchel and lays it on the table. She finds numerous comments in the margin and a paragraph-long critique on the back of the last page.

"It's a good story," he says. "As good as a lot that are published."

"Thank you," she answers, and can't help smiling as she hears what she has hoped to hear about her writing.

"Are you writing to publish or just taking up a hobby?"

"I'd really like to be able to start publishing more things. I've gotten a few things in print," she says hopefully.

"Do you know a lot about story markets?"

"No. I've never really considered different markets."

"That's an important part of publishing, knowing what magazines are looking for what. I had several stories published last year and was certain they would be published when I sent them off." Jean nods, "I guess I do need to know more about markets." "Listen, I've got a copy of the *Writer's Market* that's a couple years old. I got a new one this year, but the other is good enough to work from. You can have it if you want it."

"Thanks! Yes, I really would like to see it."

They spend another fifteen minutes talking about writing and various things, branching out to other areas of interest, to Higby's photography hobby and to Jean's collection of antiques. Then Higby stands up. "Where are you parked?"

She sits for a moment, not understanding why he needs to know this. "Come on. You can follow me over to my apartment, and I'll give you the *Writer's Market.*"

Jean looks at her watch, not sure about this, but Higby is already on his way. She catches up to him.

As she follows him across town, the day turned gray from the cloud cover, she feels giddy with anticipation, wondering what sort of apartment and furnishings Higby will have, wondering about this visit to another man's apartment that would make John furious.

Then they are there, at the apartment house, and she parks the car and looks at Higby, who stands grinning before one of the first floor units. She feels a little disappointed at seeing the place. Somehow she had expected he would live in a house with some personality, maybe have the third floor of one of the big, old homes, built for ten-member families, that cover the north end of Cranston, or have a small house of his own.

Big, cold drops of rain are falling when Jean gets out of her car, and Higby is laughing as she runs for the shelter of his apartment. She laughs, too, as she comes to the open door, and he motions for her to run on in.

The kitchen and living room are one room, a partition with a window-sized opening attempting to make it look as if there are really two. Stacks of dirty dishes are piled in the sink, and Jean gets a whiff of grease from a pan on the stove.

But the living room is clean, cluttered only with the stuff of the writer and teacher, books lying open and upside down on the coffee table, desk and bookcase, stacks of paper on the desk beside the typewriter.

Higby calls through the kitchen window, "What'll you have to drink?"

She looks at him, wondering for a moment why he should think she wants anything to drink, then says she'll have a screwdriver. He comes into the room, sits down on the edge of the couch and hands her a caramel-colored drink. "Funny looking Vodka you have here," she says.

"Bourbon and water. It's all I have, but I always ask what company wants to be polite. Let me get the book for you."

He crosses the small distance to the huge bookcase lining the end wall and kneels on the green apartment carpet, scans the bottom shelf and finally comes up with the copy. He sits down beside her again. "Look through here."

Higby takes a big slug of his drink. "The amazing thing," he says, "is that there are thousands of good writers who work years and years and never get published."

Jean nods and reaches for her drink, but by the time she has leaned back he has his arm around her shoulders and has pulled her close. She starts to jerk away, but her body does not do as she bids it, and she is kissing him back, on his lips, and feeling a tremendous surge within, feeling his beard and mustache on her face, feeling the hair over his collar. She thinks of John and pulls away.

Higby reaches for his drink and settles back once again. Jean sits forward, away from him. "Can't blame a guy for trying."

"No. I guess not."

They talk writing, but the life is gone from their discussion, and Jean makes an excuse to get away.

Chapter 15

Saturday morning Frank calls Mark on the phone he had installed after his trip to West Virginia for the funeral.

"What's happening?" Mark asks him.

"Back in town, thought I'd give you a call. Took a week's vacation to get Luke buried."

"Yeah, I'm sorry that had to happen. Where you calling from?"

"Home. Had to get a phone put in. Elly's going to stay here with me until she has the baby. A guy's going to fix my insurance card so Elly can have the baby using it. When the hospital figures things out, Elly will already be back down home." Frank laughs. "And I had to have the phone for when Elly has to go to the hospital. What's up tonight?"

"Nothing. The usual. You thinking about coming down?"

"Yeah."

"Well, come on."

He gives Frank directions to the fraternity house, and Frank says he'll be there late in the afternoon or early evening.

Most of the guys are still sleeping while Mark sits at his desk thinking. The whole thing has been a sham. Playing college is turning out to be a mistake, as he knew it would be.

But though his thoughts and the experience here at school this fall have lead Mark to confusion, there is a clarity through all of it for him now. He is here though he didn't and doesn't want to be. He is dependent on his parents once again, though only a few weeks ago he was independent of them, earning the wages on which most of Oakridge's residents can support a family. And now he knows that he must again become independent of them, must sever the economic strings that John holds on his life.

This decision reached, Mark checks his watch and sees that he will have time to get to the administration building for a refund on his tuition. He looks at the school calendar and sees that at this point in the quarter he can get a partial refund, which will amount to a pretty good grubstake. He calculates quickly before setting off for campus, and figures that with the cash in his pocket plus the refund, he will have almost four hundred dollars. Briefly, the thought enters his mind that the money is not really his but his father's, but the answer comes quickly: If John had not had him fired from his job at the carton company, he would not be in this fix.

Later, as he walks back to the house, he feels good, feels the wad of money in his wallet and its power of liberation, and knows that he is making the right decision.

When Frank arrives in the evening, Mark is in a good mood, and they sit with Pete in Mark's room passing a joint around, listening to the stereo and talking about what they might do.

Pete reaches in his shirt pocket. "This ought to make for an interesting evening," he tells them and pops one of the pills he pulled from the pocket. Frank and Mark take one each and examine it. "Should we know what it is before we take it?" Frank laughs.

"Mescaline. Organic."

Mark holds the pill in his hand, examining it. Pete and Frank sit watching him.

"What's it going to do?"

"Make you feel good."

"It's a good trip," Frank says. "I used to take it once in a while in the service. It makes you feel like, well, like you're really an important part of the world."

"What the hell," Mark finally laughs and takes it.

They sit for a half hour, Mark waiting expectantly for the thing to take hold of him, not sure what to expect, like when he had first started smoking dope in high school. They talk for a while, and then there is a subtle change as the three begin to be drawn into themselves by the drug. Mark has a tremendous rush, feels it coming on, and it is good, very good, and he smiles broadly as Pete takes the album off the stereo and switches to an FM station.

Frank looks at Mark and laughs. "Good stuff, hey?"

Mark nods in agreement, the grin stuck on his face. All through his body he can feel the smile, feel the gentleness of what is happening as his mind is led into confirming that he is all right, everything is all right with the world; and he wonders how he could have been so unhappy this fall, tries to take up his thoughts from earlier in the day, but they won't come to him, can't get past the veil of good feeling, and the rushes keep coming, more powerful, more intense, as he is led to his own personal view of the world, indeed, of the universe.

Then he hears the disc jockey announce that he is going to play an oldie requested by one of the listeners. "It's a beautiful day today," Mark hears, a little Moby Grape, and then someone is whistling the melody of the tune. "People on their way, it's a beautiful day today."

And he sinks further into the trip as the record moves through its inexorable proclamation that it's a beautiful day. And there is no doubt in Mark's mind that today is indeed a beautiful day, that there has never been a day quite like this one, that every day is beautiful, and the rushes of this beautiful day keep coming, and their intensity increases until Mark feels that he is floating, that he is capable of doing anything he wants to do.

He looks out the window and past the fence, where a stack of firewood lies in wait for winter. Next to the firewood a dog sits on the flat roof of his house staring back at Mark. Mark fixes his gaze and meets the big dog's steady stare. It is a coon hound, silky-black on top with creamy tan on his underside and legs.

Mark imagines a forest, the moon out full, the air crisp with autumn frost, the dog tracking as it was bred to do, lifting his head from the track to let out his howl of anger and excitement.

Frank says something and Pete laughs. Mark turns to face them, and they are laughing at him. "Stoned out," Pete says, and they laugh again, this time Mark along with them.

He glances back at the dog, but it is gone. In its place there is a huge, shaggy-coated bear standing on its hind legs roaring at the fraternity house. And then the bear becomes a tiger, crouching to pounce for the kill. Mark pales as the animals change, as a rattlesnake sits coiled ready to strike. Hunting coon, he thinks, trying to regain some sense of reality. Hunting. He is hunted. He feels the vulnerability of his scrawny, inadequate flesh and bone. But for a superior mind, he would still be hunted, making a meal for the bear or tiger. The dog becomes a gigantic tyrannosaurus, its long fangs dripping their lusty saliva in preparation for its attack on the fraternity house, on Mark.

He turns back to the others. Pete is swaying with the music, slapping his thigh with the beat. Frank is leaning against the wall, hands clasped behind his head, long legs dangling over the side of the bed. Mark tries to talk, glances back at the monster as it moves slowly toward them. It is in no hurry, superior in all ways to the puniness of man and his clumsy shelters. It can step on the side of the house and crush the walls, can knock over trees with its powerful arms and tail. Mark turns to the others, and finally a desperate squeak comes out of him. Pete and Frank see Mark staring wildeyed as the creature comes close. Frank jumps up and looks out the window.

"It's coming," Mark says. "We're so puny."

"What's coming?"

"Don't you see it?"

Frank kneels beside Mark and gazes out the window. He rests his arm on Mark's shoulder. "There's nothing there, man. You're imagining it all."

The dinosaur is gone, and there is the dog again, and the firewood. Mark wipes the sweat from his forehead and looks to the others.

"Let's go somewhere," Frank says to Pete.

In a few minutes they are in Pete's car. Mark feels safe now, sitting in the middle of the front seat. Whatever happens will happen to Pete or Frank first. He calms as the car glides smoothly through the streets and he watches, the many colors of the neon signs blinking their messages through the darkness to their customers, watches the masses of people on High Street.

"You okay now?" Frank asks him.

"Yeah."

"How about some women?" Pete asks. "I know some chicks in German Village. There's four of them live together in this apartment."

"Now you're talking," Frank says, laughing.

"Yeah, let's get this show on the road," Mark says, and laughs. "Wow," he says as another rush courses through him. He leans back on the seat and enjoys it.

Chapter 16

The girl who opens the door pushes it half-way closed when she sees the three of them standing there grinning. "Cindy home?" Pete asks.

"Yeah. Let me get her." She shuts the door quickly, and they can hear a bolt click.

"Nothing like the city to live in comfort and safety," Frank says.

Mark is sitting on the porch swing, moving himself back and forth with his feet, when Cindy comes to the door. She laughs. "Linda said there were three weirdos on the porch asking for me. I should have known it was you, Pete."

"Just out and around. Thought we'd stop by, unless you've already got plans."

"Come on in."

Frank and Pete step inside, and Mark, a little dizzy now, follows. The room is wood-paneled with an oval braided rug covering most of the hardwood floor. Several charcoal and watercolor sketches are spaced along the walls. "Who's the artist?" Frank asks.

Cindy calls into the other room, and in a few moments Linda has joined them, with some hastily applied eye shadow and lipstick.

"This is Linda," Cindy says. "And Pete," she says, pointing to him, "and…."

"Frank and Mark," Pete supplies and motions to them.

"You're the artist?" Frank asks her.

"I don't know if I'm an artist. But those are my

sketches."

Frank moves around the room, examining the work more closely. "Nice," he says finally, and takes the seat beside her on the couch.

Pete and Cindy are involved in some intense conversation while Frank and Linda assess each other. Mark sits in the rocker beside the front door. He can't understand how Frank and Pete can carry on so naturally. The room is a new world for him, a comfortable one, and he examines it carefully. The good feeling is back, and he is wondering why he never found out about mescaline before. It's so *good.*

"Any of your other roommates here?" Pete asks Cindy.

Mark looks at her. She is blond with fine facial features, like a magazine model would have. He looks at Linda then. She is dark, long hair down her back, her face plump.

"No," Cindy answers, and glances at Mark. "They both had dates."

Pete nods and shrugs toward Mark while Frank and Linda continue their conversation.

"We were planning to go over to the beer hall. They're kicking off the Octoberfest with dollar-a-pitcher beer tonight. Then there'll be a parade in the morning."

"Sounds alright. How about you, Mark?"

"Yeah, sure."

Cindy turns the stereo on and tunes into a rock station, lights up a joint and hands it around. Mark takes a hit when it is his turn, and passes it on. They finish it, and sit listening to the music, Mark still relaxed, leaning back in the comfortable, old rocker.

In a few minutes Mark is walking along behind the

two couples, feeling out of place. But he knows he would have nothing to say to a girl tonight, so it's just as well. He thinks for a moment of Amy, and has a rush as he steps over several gnarled, oak roots that have buckled the sidewalk. The cool air feels good on his face. The picture of him and Amy and the silver cornfield flashes through his mind, and he wishes he could see her or talk to her right now when he has the courage to tell her he loves her. At least for this moment he is sure that she is the only girl he could say he ever loved.

As they near the beer hall Mark hears the singing from within the long building. It sounds like the music that emanates from the Baptist church beside the Grotto in Oakridge, amateur voices all mixed together, garbling the words so that all that is audible from a distance is a roar.

Then they are inside, and everywhere are people carrying pitchers of beer, packed into tables, two to a seat on some chairs, row after row of beer-guzzling revelers, singing along with the accordion and piano players at the far end of the hall, the words flashed onto the wall by a slide projector. Mark feels dizzy and loses sight of the others. He finds a place to lean against the bar, the noise and activity overwhelming him. He stays there, as if paralyzed, until Frank reappears and motions for him to follow.

They sit around a small, square table that they somehow inherited. Mark watches the accordion player's fingers flitting over the keyboard. He looks at the words on the wall and realizes that most of the people are singing along. He knew they were singing when he came in, but somehow didn't notice it for a while. Strange, the tricks your mind can play on you. He wonders how much of what he sees—or better, perhaps, what he doesn't see—exists. But it doesn't matter.

He takes a huge swig and refills his cup. Then he sees the ashtray on the table. The thing is a foot square, clear glass with wet ashes in the bottom. He has never seen such a big ashtray and starts laughing. Pete and Frank laugh, too, knowing how stoned Mark is. "The ashtray," he says and starts giggling. "The biggest ashtray in the world."

The girls sit staring at him, and Pete explains.

"What an ashtray."

The evening wears on, Mark drinking with the others. He pours the beer down by habit. Frank and he, well, they drink lots of beer, he tells himself. That's what they're good at, drinking lots of beer and getting messed up.

He gets up to go to the restroom, stands unsteadily before the table and asks where it is. One of the girls points it out, and he is on his way through the crowd, saying "S'cuse me" a dozen times before he gets there. As he stands at the old trough, he feels dizzy again. More than dizzy. Nauseated, paranoid, feeling that something is drastically wrong. He feels his lunch coming up, can't stop it and leans over and pukes in the trough.

"Hey. What you doin'?"

Gagging, face red, sweat forming on his forehead, Mark lets loose another batch into the trough. "Damn," comes the voice again.

He wipes his face on the end of the cloth towel hanging out of the dispenser, wondering if he smells like puke, and unsteadily walks back to the table. The singing is loud now, and it hurts his ears. The singing and talking, the clinking of glasses. He can even hear the beer going down. He sits at the table and stares at Frank, putting his hands over his ears. "It's too loud."

Pete looks at his watch. "We better get out of here," he says, nodding at Mark. They finish their beers and Frank downs the rest of the pitcher. Outside Mark stops and leans against the wall, savoring the silence and fresh air.

This time they make Mark a part of the group as they walk. And soon Mark is laughing and joking with them again. About a block from the girls' apartment, Frank glimpses a swimming pool behind an apartment complex. "Anybody for a swim?"

"You crazy?" Pete asks. "It's cold."

But Frank is already on his way to the pool, unbuttoning his shirt. He is stripped to his underwear by the time the others catch up. There is a bicycle parked beside the pool, and Frank picks it up and carries it to the diving board. "What the hell," Pete says and strips down. As Frank rides the bike off the board, whooping a Baker laugh, Pete dives in. They splash around for a minute, the water warmer than they thought it would be. Just as they are climbing out onto the cement edge, a door opens and an angry man is shouting, "Hey! What you think you're doing?" The figure runs toward them, waving his arms and yelling. Frank and Pete scramble to pick up their clothes while Mark and the girls run for the street. The man reaches Frank as he is standing up with his clothes. "Okay. Just stay where you are. The police are on their way." He clasps Frank's arm as Frank stands up. Frank laughs as he feels the fingers slide from around his tightened biceps. He drops his clothes, picks the guy up, and holds him over his head. "Say uncle," Frank demands, laughing.

"What?"

"Say it. Say uncle."

"Uncle. Damnit," the guy says, and Frank heaves him into the pool, picks up his clothes and streaks off after the others.

Back at the girls' place, Frank sits in the living room pulling on his pants. Linda sits beside him laughing, telling him he is crazy, and Pete, laughing and trying to buckle his pants, tells about the dude Frank threw in the water.

Mark laughs along with them, then sits quietly, wondering what is going wrong. He is shaky, drained of life, afraid for some reason, but he cannot place the feeling. When the others are done laughing and carrying on, they notice Mark—two blazing eyes staring at and through everything.

Pete takes charge. "Do you have any more grass?" he asks Cindy.

"Yeah, sure."

"Mark's going to crash bad, it looks like. Can you get me a couple joints rolled?" He goes over to Mark, who is staring zombie-like from the rocker. "Listen, man. It's time we all crashed. That's what's happening right now. The dope is wearing off, the trip's over. Now we got to lie down."

Mark nods weakly and takes the joint a minute later. After a couple of hits he can feel himself relaxing, can't feel the paranoia or ugliness much at all now. After the second joint he feels drowsy and relaxes into the chair.

"You got a place where he can lie down?" Pete asks.

"Yeah. There's a room upstairs. Nobody's using it

yet. The landlord just started working on it the other day. But there's a mattress on the floor."

"Come on," Pete says to Mark, who does as instructed. "Get some sleep, and everything'll be back to normal." He follows Pete up the creaky stairs.

Mark sees the mattress in the dim light from the hallway, lies down on it and pulls a blanket over himself. He can hear the stereo from downstairs, has a few random thoughts about Amy, about his plans to become independent, but the thoughts seem unimportant now, seem far away from him. As he drifts off, he has the strange sensation that his mind and body are two different things—his body, lead heavy, his mind floating, still going full tilt, crazy characters and thoughts marching through its corridors.

Early morning, still dark, Mark hears the voices, the voice, just one, his mind tells him. The horses' hooves clang sharply against the cobblestones. Mark turns over, groggy. "Whoa," comes the voice from somewhere below. The steel horseshoes ring sharply against the stone street. Mark sits up, trying to figure out where he is, but he can't remember anything, doesn't know how he got here. The voice and hooves are real this time, no dream. He gets up and looks out the second story window at the brick alley below. He glimpses the horses and a wagon, a banner saying something about October on the back of it. How did he get here? How long has he lived here? Frantically Mark goes to the door and opens it, but there is only a closet. He looks around the room, the light from the alley illuminating it just enough for him to find the other door. He tries to open it, but it doesn't give, the old doorjamb swelled tight against the door. He gropes along the wall, feeling for a light switch, tries to call for help, but hears himself whimper. He clicks the light on finally, and blinks against the brightness of the bare bulb.

Then he sees it, this green room from his dreams, dirty-green, decayed wallpaper drooping pieces of itself here and there. In one corner are piled plaster and scraps of rotten wallpaper. The voice, horses, room, this place of sickness and death. He tries to call out again, then runs for the door. He tumbles into the hallway and against another door, and then the tears come big and hot as he looks into the green room.

The door by his head opens quickly, and Frank is standing there in his underwear. Frank kneels beside him as Linda appears in the doorway wrapped in a blanket. "What's the matter, man?"

"I lived here. I died in that room." Pete and Cindy have joined them now, and they all stand around Mark, his chest heaving, gasping for air. Cindy kneels down with Frank, and Mark reaches for her, puts his arms around her neck. She doesn't resist, though he is holding her so tightly it hurts, but lays her head on his convulsing   chest.

Chapter 17

The richness of life— if only you let it happen. No guilt about being hungry and finding someone to take away the hunger. She ran the day he kissed her, ran through the rain, carrying her jacket, jumped into her car and was gone.

Jean sits at her desk, trying to get her mind off Higby and back to the plotting of her novel. She already has fifteen pages of synopsis, and after it is complete, will begin a chapter-by-chapter outline, just as Higby advised her to do.

She pictures Thursday in class, she and Higby not looking at each other, both a little bewildered by the day before. She sees John, too, on Thursday night, shaky nervous again for some reason, impotent. They always had a good sex life, but now there is nothing. It hurts her to think of being happy with Higby, her only lover since her marriage, when John is so troubled. But she can't help herself.

She looks at the papers. Higby told her he would help. Step by step he would help her write her first book. But she drifts back into her daydream again. It is so pleasant to sit and feel the way she does now, thinking ahead to the coming week. They can love every day if they want.

Friday in class. And then after class she manages to meet him at the door, and he stops to let her out ahead of him. In the hall, then, "I forgot the book Wednesday. Can I stop by and get it this afternoon?" Higby has appointments for the next hour. "See you about three-thirty?" she says and turns and walks away, Higby standing there in the hall watching her as she heads for the stairway, then turning to go to his office as the message sinks in.

John emerges from the bedroom, just showered and shaved. "Leaving now," he calls to Jean from the kitchen. "What time did you say you were coming out?"

"About three. Millie and I are playing tennis."

"We can eat about six."

She hears the door close and listens as the car glides down the driveway. Golf and work, she thinks. Golf and work and not a new thought in fifteen years, not a new thing about him. She feels guilty again, but only for a moment. Higby treats her so much better. It's different. And exiting.

Higby opening the door at her knock. "What'll you have to drink?" Screwdriver, she says and waits as he mixes the bourbon and water. He lays the book on the table before the couch and sits down, waiting. It's her show. Could I see the rest of your apartment? Sure. She follows him into the only part of the place she hasn't seen, the bedroom. You want to see the closets? They laugh. Clothes strewn around the bedroom floor, a manuscript on the dresser. He turns around, and she reaches for him, and they kiss.

The golf course is the only thing that keeps John going these days, the only part of his life that feels right. He hits the ball, watches it bounce and roll the extra yards because of his slight hook, goes for distance, for the pin every shot, chips and putts with a fierce concentration, blotting out his conscious mind and its ever-present slide show of the wreck.

It's over, and he's free, no one will ever suspect that John Holz, the man who sells machined parts and makes an honest living at it, is a killer. Time will pass and ease the thoughts, he knows. It's today he can't handle.

John is on the putting green, practicing as the groups ahead of him tee off. He bought a new putter, one with the thinner blade. Hard as the greens are, he doesn't need the mallet.

He watches as the lightly tapped ball rolls toward the hole on the far side of the green. "Ready, John?" calls Bill Blatt, who is standing near the tee with Gary Cooper. Gary is off first. John looks around. "Where's Jerry?"

Bill shrugs as he steps onto the tee. "Didn't show. He can join us on the course when he gets here."

Then it is John's turn, and he stands addressing the ball. He has a mental picture of Jerry and Jean the way he saw them last week, thoroughly enjoying each other's company. Could there be anything between them? His hands are shaking slightly, and he steps back and takes another practice swing. Blot it. Blot it out. The hands are steady, then, and he sees nothing but the persimmon club face of his driver resting behind the new Titleist, feels nothing but the smooth, grooved swing and stands watching his drive as it climbs on its trajectory, as it peaks and begins to drop, hits between the bunkers that mark 240 yards from the tee.

They are walking today, as they do every so often for the exercise, Bill pulling his bag on a cart, John and Gary carrying theirs on their shoulders. John plans his next shot, looking at the flag to see where it is placed today, and already has his wedge out of his bag while he waits for Bill to take his second shot.

Mark sits in Frank's pickup, most of his belongings loaded in the back, his stereo in boxes on the front seat between him and Frank. Mark is strung out and embarrassed at the spectacle he made last evening, his mind functioning in ways he never knew possible, and is glad that the boxes serve as a partition between him and Frank. He wants to be alone, needs time to think, let the confusion of last night subside, get rid of the anxiety that has plagued him all morning. Loading his belongings in the truck was a trial in itself. Here he is going back to the place he meant to get away from, back to Mommy and Daddy, he tells himself as they ride through the after-church traffic in Cranston. If he weren't so strung out, he might have taken off hitch-hiking for the West, anything, anywhere. Nothing like messing things up again. He'll have to hack it with them until he can find a job and a place to stay.

He can't even laugh at Frank's satirical monologue as they move down First Street past the mansions and stately homes of the doctors, lawyers and executives of Cranston. "And here is Doctor Boner's residence," Frank is saying. "If you look out the right side of the bus, you will see his home through the trees, down the quarter mile concrete driveway. Doctor Boner is known mainly for two things: he has one of the longest driveways in the world, equal in value to the average price of homes in this country, and he has the record for performing the most appendectomies in a one year period. On the approaching curve lives attorney Ralph Reamer."

Frank sees that Mark is not getting into it, not like he usually does when they get to laughing and carrying on, mocking and laughing. He leans forward and looks over at Mark. "Thought maybe you fell out a ways back."

Mark manages a weak smile. "Give it a day, man," Frank tells him. "It'll go away. I took some acid once, and it did the same thing to me. Felt really bad for a day or two. The old head pulled some strange stuff on me, but it quit. Get some sleep. Have a couple drinks of your old man's heavy-duty stuff, take the edge off."

Mark knows Frank is right. He's just strung out, knows his head is still together, just has to get over the little bit of leftover bummer. But he's been on so many bummers lately, he doesn't have the energy to pull himself out of this one right away. He pictures his old man breathing fire because he quit school, his mother concerned about *why* he quit.

"Dead man's curve ahead," Frank says as they approach the curve where Luke was killed.

Mark sits up and watches as they enter it. "How can you joke about it?"

"Not sure I was joking."

Jean puts her book down as she hears Frank's truck in the driveway. She holds the door as Mark approaches. "What are you doing?"

"Can I keep my things here for a few days?"

"Of course. But why, what happened?"

"Quit school," he says as he heads for his room.

Then Frank walks by with an armload of things, nodding at Jean. She follows them back the hallway. Frank slips by her, but Mark stops. She stares at him, incredulous.

He looks at her deeply tanned, fine-featured face, and she meets his gaze and sees the fear and bewilderment in his eyes. "Can we talk later?" he says and is already moving around her. As they are finishing the unloading, she catches Frank alone in the kitchen. "What happened?" she demands.

"How do you mean?" Frank says and rests the box of books against the counter.

"You know what I mean," she snaps. "Every time you're around, there's trouble. Now what's the matter with Mark?"

Frank shrugs. "Little too much partying is all."

Mark hears the end of the conversation. "Come off it, Mom. I'm old enough to dig my own grave."

Frank continues on his way. "Are you sick?"

"Yeah, sick, just want to lie down a while. Hung over bad," he says and avoids looking at her.

"And you quit school?"

He glances at her, wishes he had not come back here, and goes outside to get the last load. Frank comes back into the kitchen. "You stay the hell away from him," Jean hisses as he pulls open the screen door. Frank looks at her, shrugs and walks out. Jean watches as Mark and Frank stand leaning against the truck's tailgate talking. Then Frank is gone.

"Do you want some coffee?" Jean asks Mark when he is back inside.

"Just want to rest," he says, and she follows him to his room.

"But what's the matter?"

"Just leave me alone," he says as he flops onto his bed. Jean stands in the doorway for a few moments, closes the door quietly and returns to the kitchen, where she puts the tea kettle on. Waiting for the water to boil, she looks through the book she was reading, *The Grapes of Wrath.* Wherever she turns in the book, she finds nothing but struggle, the Joads limping westward in their dilapidated, old truck, people dying and starving, being clubbed to death by guards, chased here and there by the cotton and citrus growers. But she keeps thinking of Mark. Why should he struggle so? What does he have to struggle for? Why should he torment himself the way he has this summer and fall when all he has to do is ride things out, get his degree, find a good job. And John. What is he struggling with? They have everything they could possibly need, no hunger, can have nearly anything there is to be had in the world. What would things be like for them if they had no money, no house or car or food? Would they be close like the Joad family, loving and caring instead of streaking blindly around the way they are? If they had nothing but themselves? She wonders what Mark would be like if he had not always had so much.

The tea kettle whistles, slicing the quiet of the house.

Chapter 18

John stands looking ahead to the eighteenth green, holding his seven-iron, chopping at weeds that have outgrown the grass since the last mowing. Bill's shot comes off the side of the clubface, hits on top of the hill and bounces into the rough. John is disgusted—he's told Blatt a hundred times to keep his right hand on top so he won't be shanking the ball all the time.

John walks slowly back to his ball and watches as Gary lays into his shot. Kid'll make a decent golfer, another year or two of serious practice, John thinks as he stands addressing his ball. Jerry never showed, didn't call, nothing. Where could he be? Gertrude in Cleveland with Jenny, their daughter, just had her first baby and Grandma up to help. Jerry alone somewhere? On Sunday? John goes a little deep, takes too much divit, but gets some distance anyway. Might be in the trap though. Heck of a way to finish a round.

The eighteenth hole. Either play another nine by himself or head to the watering trough with the rest of the golfers, swill down a few with the guys. And then what? More of the same, feeling something wrong inside but not knowing what to do about it, feeling nauseated all the time.

His ball is in the sand trap as he expected, but he doesn't care, takes out his sand wedge, blasts it out and hits the green. Has to settle for a bogey. In a few minutes they are walking the cinder path to the pro shop, Bill and Gary chatting about their round. "Buy you a drink," Bill says to John.

Forced to decide. "I think I'll play another round. Not much good weather left this year. You want to play along?" he asks, knowing that they never play more than eighteen. John looks at his watch. It's only three o'clock. He can take his electric cart out and be back in by four-thirty, about the time Jean will be finished playing tennis.

"What are you going to do? Turn pro?" Bill asks him.

"Already have a good job."

Gary veers away from them to the parking lot to put his clubs in his car. "See you in a little bit," he calls.

"Okay. Good game," John says. Bill stands with John as he uncovers his cart and straps his bag onto the back of it. Bill knows, has sensed in the past weeks, that something is wrong. He got a call last week from the shipping foreman. "Holz had better get off me," he told Bill. "I can't ship what I don't have. If he wants orders shipped before they're on the dock, tell him to come out here and run the place himself." Something is wrong. Bill watches the grim look of determination on John's face. The man can't relax anymore. "What's been happening, John?"

John finishes strapping the bag. "How do you mean?"

Bill shrugs, not sure how to approach the subject. John has been loyal and hard-working for twenty years, never needing any criticism. "Something's bugging you. It shows."

John wipes the sweat from his forehead, sits down on the cushioned seat, knowing he has to come up with something. Only one thing: "That accident I was in. It just keeps coming back. I guess that has to be it."

"But it wasn't your fault. Why let it bother you?"

John grips the steering wheel and stares ahead.

"Yeah. It's just hard to shake." He looks up at Bill. "You know, something like that happens, you wonder if maybe you could have avoided it somehow, maybe gone in the ditch or something, anything."

"Sure you want to go another nine?" Bill asks, starting towards the garage door of the proshop.

"Yeah. It helps more than anything."

Bill flashes the okay sign.

The driver, ball, fairway, wide open space of the now-deserted course. The ball cracks against the clubface, and John is on his way.

Jean cancelled her tennis date with Millie in order to stay home with Mark. Maybe she and John shouldn't have pushed him into going back to school. But it is so simple, she keeps telling herself. All Mark has to do is get motivated about school, get out of the rut that the factory seemed to put him in this summer. The factory and Frank. Nothing but trouble with him. Some kind of freak, she thinks, halfway intelligent, but not a value in him, values nothing more than having a good time. She knows about him, did some checking after Mark went back to school. Talked to Caldwell from National Carton one evening at the club. Troublemaker, he told her. Caused the strike. Nothing but trouble, comes back to work half drunk sometimes after lunch, but the union won't let us fire him, he told Jean. Stick up for him. Going to fire him this winter, though, try again when work is slow, and it won't hurt us to lose a couple of weeks of production. Make it stick this time. Nothing but trouble. Damn hillbilly.

Mark sleeps all afternoon. At eight o'clock when

Jean checks him, Mark is sitting on the edge of his bed. "Want to talk?" she asks as she sits down beside him. He shakes his head no. "Are you hungry?" No again. "I don't want to pry," she says. "Just know that I'm here whenever you need me."

Just what he didn't need to hear. Mommy's here for him, will drop everything to tend after him and his propped-up happiness, like she is propping up the clothesline in the back yard where she hangs her sheets out to dry. Makes them smell like the sun and wind she always says. And Daddy will give you money so you can be happy. "I don't want any help," he says quietly. "I'm twenty years old."

"I was only trying to help."

"I'll be downstairs," he says as he gets up and walks around a pile of his clothes lying in the middle of the floor. Jean stays behind and starts hanging the clothes in his closet.

Mark turns on the TV in the basement rec room, gets a coke out of the fridge and sits back in the leather chair. He watches the last few plays of a football game, then turns off the set as the announcer comes on to report the rest of the action in the nation's football stadiums. At the pool table he racks the balls and breaks, wondering what future civilizations will think of our huge coliseums left over from this mass culture. Maybe they'd all be rusted away, though, inferior as they are to Rome's arenas. Yeah, the whole culture will rust away in a hundred years with nobody around to paint it and rustproof it. Cars rusted to red dust on the streets of the cities, factories falling down as their steel support beams rot away, housing forming piles of sawdust with pieces of aluminum siding lying like huge garbage bag ties over the mess.

He cues the ball too hard to be accurate and gives it up. Back in the chair he picks up a *Sports Illustrated* and reads an article about jogging, looks through an old *Time* with its depressing array of world news. He puts the magazine down and thinks again of the green room. The puzzle, the head game of dreams, becoming real.

He goes upstairs, and Jean turns away from the stove as she hears him. "Sloppy joes. They'll be ready in a few minutes."

"I'm not hungry," he tells her and stands uncertainly for a moment. "Can I use your car?"

"Sure." She digs her keys out of her purse.

Mark has been gone only a short time when the phone rings. "Where you been?" comes a voice that she doesn't recognize.

"Who is this?"

"What the hell you mean, who is this?"

"John, what's the matter?"

"You and Jerry have a good time today?" he blurts out, his subconscious burned to the surface by the drinks he has had.

"Will you quit with this stuff?" she says in disgust. "You're drunk, John. Please come home."

"You and Jerry have a good...." She slams the receiver down. *What* in *hell* is happening. All this nonsense about her and Jerry. Where could John have gotten such an idea? She dials Jerry's number, meaning to ask him if John has said anything to him about their "affair." After a minute she hangs up in disappointment. She sits thinking of John's mental state and is frightened. He is changing so rapidly; something is wrong. The newspaper, she suddenly thinks. Maybe

Jerry had to work for some reason today. She dials the number quickly and listens to the hollow ring, ready to hang up when Jerry answers.

"Jerry, this is Jean. I'm so glad I found you. There's something I need to talk to you about."

"Sure."

"How come you're working today?" she asks, her curiosity momentarily overcoming her need to tell him about John.

"Fired the layout man Friday." He sighs into the receiver. "Been working all day getting most of tomorrow's edition ready. Showing one of the girls how to do the job." He sounds tired.

"You remember when we talked about John, you know, him thinking that there was something going on between us?"

"Yeah, sure. I never have been able to figure it out."

"Well, he just called from the club. He started in about us again, thinking that we were together today." Jerry is silent. "Has he said anything to you about it?"

"Not a word. Never a thing. He's hinted around about some problems between you and him, but never included me in them."

"I'm scared, Jerry. There's something wrong with him."

"I've noticed a big difference lately. He's quieter than usual." He waits for her response, but it doesn't come, and finally he asks her if she's still there.

"Yes. I was just thinking." Another pause.

"Listen, Jean, can we finish this tomorrow? I've got another hour's work to do here, and it's been a long day."

"The irony of the whole thing is," she starts off,

ignoring what Jerry said, "that I *am* seeing someone else. The way John's been lately."

"What? Why would you tell me something like that? I don't want to know that! Damnit, I thought I knew you better than that."

"I just thought I could...." She stops, realizing the error she has made. "I shouldn't have told you. It just came out. I thought we could talk."

"I've got to get to work. Some other time." And he hangs up.

Jean sits looking at the scattered papers of her book plans. Why did she tell Jerry that she was seeing someone? Divorce at the very least if John finds out. But the way things have been going, a divorce might not be so bad anyway. There is Higby, her writing, her life, which has been stifled long enough. She has given and given in her marriage. It just has to be her turn to feel alive,   to   explore,   feel   good   about   life.

Chapter 19

Higby sits at the long upholstered bar in the Reno Lounge watching Linda do her bump and grind to the music from the jukebox. Tired tonight. He turns back to his beer and pours another glass. Got about three thousand words today. He sat for an hour or so in the morning, trying to figure the best way to open the next chapter. Drank a pot of coffee and was on his way. Three thousand words, good words.

He watches Linda, waiting for her to be finished. Things are finally shaping up for him in Cranston. Linda's a good woman and now there's this other one, Jean. He smiles as he thinks of her: hungry, stepping out for the first time in years, though he wishes she wouldn't confide so much about her troubles with her husband. Hell, he's not a psychiatrist.

The song over, Linda sits beside him. "Thought you weren't coming," she says.

Higby motions for the bartender to give her a beer. "Had a lot of work for school to get caught up on. You know, grading papers and stuff."

"Yeah," she says and scoots her bar stool closer so their legs touch. "All that work, teaching and everything. Aren't many people smart enough to do that."

Higby laughs. "Most people could do what I do."

She looks at him cocking her head slightly, looking sideways out of pouty eyes, lips puckered a little. He laughs. It is the same quizzical expression that attracted him to her in the first place. Sat down at the bar, second time he'd been in the place, and here comes the go- go girl whose body he's been admiring, comes and sits down beside him. Nice bod, nice dance, he told her. And then the sidelong glance that cracked him up. Bought her a couple of drinks then, arranged to pick her up at midnight.

"Don't be putting me on," she says.

They have a couple more beers while another girl takes over for the rest of the slow Sunday evening, and soon Higby is following Linda to her apartment.

Mark sits on the bank of the reservoir where he and Amy were only a few weeks before. So much has happened since then, it seems, so much more than he is capable of understanding. It's been hard, trying to figure out who or what he is. He thinks of Amy. Her beauty is in his mind. The clean scent of her hair comes to him. But she isn't there.

A tree limb sticks out of the water ten or fifteen yards from shore, and he wonders how a tree ended up there. He stares at it a long while. A tree accidentally in a reservoir. Mark Holz accidentally looking at the limb on a Sunday night, sitting in a car that someone accidentally invented over the ages. Splat! goes the sperm against the wrinkled wall, and lo and behold, the accident of conception, billions of accidents creating beings who are all different, all accidentally here now because of what? What the hell is this? Why does it have to be the way it is? So many accidental happenings. Even the thoughts are accidental. He can't control them, has no idea where their ugly procession begins, where it is coming from or where it is headed.

He pictures Amy again. How good it would be to have her hug him right now, to hold him tight and let him know that he is not alone.

He is conscious of the radio. It's been on all the time, but he didn't seem to hear it until now. Strange. So strange the way the conscious mind works, able to focus only on one or two things at a time. He listens to the rich female voice as it states, "I want to be free." He gets out of the car and sits on the fender, looking out over the water.

A grove of pines stretches before him and up a steep hill. He moves to them and stands in the midst of their darkness and tarry scent. Looking up to the star-studded sky, he moves his head back and forth and wonders at the movement of the stars and heavens with his own movement, feels that he is the center of the universe, and the oneness that he felt last night with the mescaline wraps him, the knot forming again in his stomach as he remembers.

He runs through the trees, still looking upward to the heavens. A tree branch slaps his face, and he tears at the limb savagely, cursing it. Needles shed off into his hands, but the limb is too stout for him to break. He stops and gazes at the stars again. "Take me with you!" he shouts. He runs and falls over a stick, and lies on the bed of pine needles.

The roar of a car engine startles him, and then comes the squealing of tires as the car and its lovers speed away from this madman from the pines. The smell of burning rubber and dust is in the air and Mark sits up, the anger and fright beginning to subside.

Amy again. He will call her when he gets home, tell her he is coming for her, that he'll be there tomorrow to see her. Vague plans form in his mind as he drives home. Got to get a job tomorrow. Find a room somewhere. Will go home and call Amy.

In the basement Jean waits for Mark to come home. She dreads it, knows that John is going to be nasty. She hears one of the kitchen chairs being slid across the floor above her. Then the thump against the door as John barricades it with the chair. Then comes his laugh, and she scrambles up the stairs and tries to open the door. She pushes, lunges with all her might. John laughs louder as he listens to her scratching and thumping against the door, laughs at this joke on his unfaithful wife, and mixes himself another drink. She stands at the top of the stairs, listening to John tramping around the house. Into Mark's room, back to the kitchen. Back and forth, thumping, dropping things on the kitchen floor.

"Hey!" she hears then. "Joe College! How's it goin'?"

She hears the kitchen door close. "Come on, buddy. Goin' to college tonight. Got everything packed up for you."

Mark stands in amazement, his belongings spread over the kitchen floor. Seeing John's numb face and red eyes, Mark shakes his head slowly back and forth, and walks over to right his stereo turntable, which lies upside down where John dropped it. Mark lifts the arm, and it comes off in his hand.

"Aw, no problem. We'll get a new one," John says. "Come on, now, you get my car, and we'll get started loading up. Goin' to college."

Mark stands dumbly, shakes his head again. Can't talk, nothing to talk *about* now.

Jean bangs on the door and calls to Mark to let her out. He starts slowly for the door.

"I said get the car!"

Mark pulls the chair away. Why is this happening? he asks himself as he turns back to John. But the old man is there waiting, grabs his shirt and pulls, nearly causing both of them to fall, rights himself and slaps Mark's face. His head snaps to the left, the expressionless face twisting with the punch. Jean bursts into the kitchen as John backhands Mark. Mark stands calmly, blankly, looking for his father's eyes, but they are hidden by the red glaze of alcohol and anger. Jean moves quickly past them and picks up a cast iron frying pan. But John lets Mark go, stands staring at his motionless form, turns slowly away in bewilderment and wanders into the den, taking small, shuffling steps.

Mark stands watching his father retreat, the warm metallic taste of blood in his mouth. Jean puts the pan down and tries to hug him, but he pushes her away and goes to his bedroom. She follows and watches as he falls onto his bed. His head twisted sharply, John lies passed out on the couch, snoring grotesquely, huge inhalations flapping through his throat.

In the living room, Jean sits sadly on the couch. There is nothing she can do to right this wreck of a home. Before retiring, she checks Mark. The hall light shows his face as she kneels to kiss his cheek, the dried blood black on his mouth and pillow. She sees now that she cannot help him. He no longer has need for a mother.

Chapter 20

The eyes open slowly, puffy and unsure of what they are seeing.

John lies for several minutes, wondering how he ended up in the den, unable to move without stirring up the pain in his head. He shields his eyes as the sun comes momentarily from behind a cloud and bursts in through the picture window.

He sits on the edge of the couch and massages his temples, feeling the raw roof of his mouth with his swollen tongue. He lurches to his feet. Mark's clothes, books, and stereo scattered over the kitchen floor surprise him. The shock of memory comes slowly upon him, painful in its fuzziness. Mark back home. Jean locked in the basement. He goes to the basement door, and looks down the dark stairway. He shuts the door, goes to the refrigerator and takes a long drink of juice from the carton.

Finding Jean's stash of codeine in her desk, he takes a couple pills. God almighty. He stands leaning against the counter, surveying the mess. Then he remembers slapping Mark. He moans inwardly, ashamed because he has hurt the people who mean the most to him, afraid because he let himself do it. He is no longer in control.

Fighting the nausea back, he enters the bedroom and stands looking at Jean for a moment, then quietly from the closet takes the first suit he comes to, slips a shirt from a wire hanger and a tie from the rack. In the half-bath off the den he stands looking in the mirror at the wreck that is John Holz. He splashes water on his face, brushes his teeth, and dresses quickly, holding on to the sink to steady himself as he pulls on his trousers. He doesn't look in the mirror again.

In the garage he looks at his watch. Only seven o'clock. He groans aloud. An hour early for work. What will he do there this early in the morning? Work, dummy, he tells himself. Work, get lost in the busy-work of the week.

None of the office help is in yet, and John is glad for this; he knows he looks like he feels, and at least nobody will witness his dishevelment. He makes a pot of coffee and sits in the seclusion of his office savoring the hot stuff. His ulcer is kicking up and he responds by taking a hit of Maalox and drinking a second cup of coffee.

Feeling better, he rummages through the bottom desk drawer until he finds the electric razor. When he steps out of the rest room a few minutes later, slightly more presentable now as confirmed by a look in the mirror, he is startled by the "Good morning" from the office secretary.

"Morning," he says, and the girl gazes after him as he hurries into his office and shuts the door.

Jean wakes with a start at eight-thirty. The evening comes vividly back as she checks Mark. Still asleep. She goes to wake John for work. He'll be late, but she might as well get him going, get him out of the house so she can try to talk to Mark. She stands wondering how he managed to get out of the house without her hearing him. But it doesn't matter. The thought of seeing him disgusts her.

Jean has coffee and her usual soft-boiled egg and

starts cleaning up the debris from the kitchen floor. Later, ready to leave for school, she thinks of waking Mark, not knowing he has lain in bed listening to her roam the house. When she looks in on him, he closes his eyes. He doesn't want to see her or John. When she is gone, he gets up and has a cup of leftover, lukewarm coffee.

The sun comes and goes, huge gray clouds moving rapidly through the skies, promising either a clear day or more clouds and rain. Mark watches out the window for a while, watches as the clouds, the world, people go on their way without him.

He's got to be doing something. Getting a job, finding a place to live. Anywhere will do, he tells himself as he washes his face. If you don't have a home, you can't do any worse, no matter where you live. But when he comes out of the bathroom, he realizes he is helpless. How is he going to go anywhere to get a job or find a room when he has no car and little money? And there aren't many jobs anyway.

He finds himself looking through the junk drawer in the kitchen, sifting through the remains of decades— things that he and Jean and John could not bring themselves to throw away for one reason or another. Clay marbles, pocket knives, grade school pictures, a reed whistle his grandfather gave him one year for his birthday, a toy cap pistol, a small alarm clock that folds up in a leather case. He picks up the gun and points it out the window at the neighbor's cat as it stalks a bird in the back yard. "Bang," he says, wishing he had a real gun. Teach these domestic cats a thing or two.

He goes to the basement, not looking for anything in particular, simply exploring his former life here, a time when he was happy and worry-free. In one corner of the basement, on the unfinished side where the washer and drier sit, Mark stands before his old "laboratory." Chemicals on a shelf. Test tubes, eye droppers, a garter snake and a mouse preserved in formaldehyde. He marvels at the fineness of the mouse's fur and the many colors of the snake's skin, preserved from so many years ago. When he had wanted to be a doctor. Or rather, John and Jean had wanted him to be one, convinced him by the time he was twelve that he wanted to be a medical man. Of course, that was before they discovered that he had no aptitude for science and mathematics. He wanted to be a lawyer then, they told him. In the ceramic cabinet in the corner he finds the fishing poles and tackle that he and John once used.

In the woods behind the house he digs through the leafy humus for worms. Soon he is walking toward the end of the street, toward the pond where he and John used to go fishing on Saturday mornings so many years ago. And he pictures the little boy and the big, strong father. Where'd they go? They no longer exist. Nothing is the same anymore, nothing feels right now, as time carries Mark along in its rough wake.

John sits in the waiting room and lights a cigarette, thinking how he will go about telling Doctor Branscom about his problem. His cigarette fouls the clean air of the room, and he snubs it out, feeling guilty.

Then the nurse smiles at him from the hallway to the examining rooms: "Mr. Holz." He follows her to one of the rooms, and she motions for him to sit down. "What can we do for you, Mr. Holz?"

He is surprised—he hadn't thought of having to tell the nurse anything. "Just not feeling too good lately. Thought I'd come in for a checkup."

When the doctor is finally with him, John is wishing he hadn't come here. He never could understand why Branscom didn't belong to the country club. Hell, he plays golf; one of his kids was on the high school golf team when Mark was, but the doc plays at the public course, which is always crowded with hackers, making for slow play.

"I'm not sure," John says finally as the doctor waits. "My nerves seem to be shot lately. Tense, thinking rotten things. And I'm drinking way too much."

"Which comes first, the cart or the horse?"

"What?"

"Do you think your nerves are causing you to drink, or your drinking is causing the tension?"

"Several weeks ago I was in an accident. A man was killed. That has a lot to do with it, I think. But other things may be a part of it too."

The doctor stands looking at John's chart. "How about your ulcer? Acting up again?"

"Yeah," John says, having forgotten about it as he concentrated on trying to explain his problem. "Been bothering me lately."

"There's two ways to go about this. We can put you in the hospital for a couple of days and run a complete physical, see what's going on inside, or I can give you a prescription for a tranquilizer to calm you down some. But anything I prescribe cannot be mixed with alcohol."

"What would you rather have me do?"

"I think it would be good to have you in the hospital. You can get started on the medication and at the same time get a complete workup."

John nods slowly, considering. "Okay. You're the doc. When do you want me there?"

"I think we can get a bed for you tomorrow morning. We'll have Marge call them right now and see how things look."

As John leaves the office, scheduled to be at the hospital next morning at eleven o'clock, he already feels better and decides to take the rest of the day off.

At home John replaces his suit with slacks and a golf shirt and in a half hour has teed off. The club, the ball, the hole. That's all he needs for the rest of the day.

The pond is in a field a quarter mile from the nearest road, beyond the edge of the property that comprised the farm John Holz bought many years before and sold off to home builders. Mark walks slowly toward a fence that has been put up since his last visit to the pond. "No Fishing" states a hand-painted, red-enamel-on -white sign hanging on the fence.

The clouds are gone now, and the fall sun is warm, the sky deep blue to the horizons. After climbing the fence, Mark gazes across the field. A hawk soars overhead, waiting for a rabbit or mouse to betray itself with movement.

Mark walks slowly toward the pond. He descends a slight grade and stops and looks again. No houses or roads in sight now, just the sun and the sky, the weeds of the field full of life, bees and butterflies making the rounds of weed blossoms, grasshoppers springing here and there, leaving the brittle weeds shaking. Birds flitting about in the growth of trees near the pond.

"It's beautiful," he says softly. How has he missed

seeing this part of the world for so long, seeing beyond the materials of civilization? Mark looks up again and notices that as the blue sky stretches to its horizons, a haze is accumulated. He drops the fishing pole and lies down on the bed of weeds. There must be one spot, he thinks, where the sky is bluest. He searches for it, feeling alive and powerful in this discovery of the sky's blueness. He watches the bluest spot and unbuckles his belt and slides his faded jeans to his knees. The grass is warm and soft beneath him. He watches that bluest spot and it is his.

He lies there in the field, feels the healing and restoration within the release, and wonders if the animals of the world have such a difficult time of things as people do. And he knows that they don't, that they breed and perpetuate themselves and die off, with no thought of anything but the moment, the surviving. How weak humans are compared to the fertile and automatic ways of the natural world, of this field and pond, how difficult and complicated for man to even exercise his fertility.

Chapter 21

Back home, Mark thinks of his bicycle in the garage, and after pumping up the tires and finding that they hold air, is on his way, exhilarated at finding this long-forgotten piece of transportation to solve his problems of getting around.

He rides slowly, dry leaves swirling down around him from the maples and beeches, the sun still warm. Things are all right. Today is good, and he can't believe the many changes and feelings of the last twenty-four hours. Many bad, yet now hope is with him again. As he enters Oakridge, on a whim he stops at the Shell station, the place where his family has traded for years. He parks his bike by the tall glass doors of the garage and waits for Walt to finish servicing a car at the far island. "Hey, Walt. How's it going?" Mark greets him.

"Okay. Can't complain. Nobody will listen anyways." Walt takes off to service another customer, and Mark waits patiently. In a few minutes he's back. "Beautiful day," Walt says. "Just out taking a ride?"

"Sort of. Looking for a job and I thought I'd stop by and see if you needed any help."

Walt looks him up and down. "You serious? Aren't you going to school anymore? Your dad was in the other day, said you were in Columbus."

"Nah. I quit. Tired of the rat race."

"Yeah, I got a place open. Nights, though. Don't pay a whole lot. You know anything about working on cars? There's usually a couple of oil changes, grease jobs, tires to fix, stuff like that for the evening when it gets slow."

"I can learn all that. Give me a few days."

"You sure? Only pays $2.25 an hour. Couple of months you'll get two fifty, but that's tops."

"I need a job."

"Okay, let's do the paperwork." The bell rings as another car pulls in for gas, and Walt motions to the man in the lube bay to come out. The forms filled out, Walt asks Mark when he can start.

"Tomorrow?"

"Good enough. Be here around three. Regular shift will be three-thirty to eleven-thirty. Show you a few things before we turn you loose on the pumps."

"Thanks, Walt," Marks says as he climbs back on his bicycle. "See you tomorrow."

Walt waves quickly as he heads toward the car on the lift in the lube bay. Better than some dirtball, he is thinking as he picks up the grease gun. Least the kid ought to be able to make change without losing money.

Class over, Jean and Higby stay behind to talk, and decide to have coffee so he can look over the beginnings of her novel. Higby reads through the synopsis quickly, too fast, it seems to Jean, for him to do justice to it. Occasionally, he stops and writes in the margins. They discuss the next step: the chapter by chapter outline. Jean nods, taking in all he is saying, watching his fine-featured face as he looks over the pages for a second time. He's so much different than John. In command, not angry all the time or unreasonable. "Want to finish at my place?" he asks after their second cup of coffee.

Whoosh. The swing, the ball and its trajectory, a good shot. Then the cart racing after the ball, and John takes his next shot, hits the green, and is pleased, more relaxed than he has been for weeks. The golf today, the hospital tomorrow. As much as he hates hospitals, he is glad to be going in. Get him out of things for a few days, see what new damage he has inflicted by his latest binges. He'll have nothing to do but lie around and let them take care of him, though he is not looking forward to the upper and lower x-rays, all the enemas they'll pump into him tomorrow night to clean out his system and prepare it for the barium milkshakes.

Mark feels strange parking a bicycle behind the Grotto. The place is nearly empty, only a few people sitting along the bar. He gets a beer, sits down in one of the booths, and spreads a newspaper out. There is only one furnished apartment advertised, and the rent is a hundred and fifty a month—more than he can pay.

Then he sees the "furnished rooms" ad: "by the week or month," and since the place is only a few blocks from the bar, he drains his beer and sets off on his bike.

An old woman answers his knock and gives him a quick looking- over.

"How much are the rooms?"

"Twenty-five a week, ninety a month." She stares at him while waiting for his answer.

"Price sounds okay." He stands waiting for her to open the door. "Could I look at one?"

She comes out and holds the porch rail, letting herself down one step at a time onto her thick ankles. Mark walks slowly behind as she hobbles along. A stairway leads up the side of the old wood house. She points up the stairs. "Second one on the right."

Mark finds himself in a dark hallway. He can't locate a light switch and has to wait for his eyes to adjust. Then he is in the room. The first thing he notices is the bright green wallpaper, which is splotched with one-inch yellow circles enclosing small red dots. Like a thousand pairs of eyes watching him. Weird. The place is clean, a single bed and mattress in one corner, and a table made from a wood door with two-by-fours for legs sitting before the window. An easy chair with stuffing hanging out its wounded side is in another corner. There is a big closet. He can put his stereo on the table. It looks all right. He can live here. He steps back into the hall and walks to the other end. An antique Frigidaire sits purring on one side, and a door across from it opens onto the toilet and shower. He counts the rooms on the way out. Five, including his.

The old woman stands at the bottom of the stairs, holding the rail for support. "I'll take it for a month," he says. She turns, makes her way back to the porch and disappears into the house. In a few minutes she returns with a paper in her hand. "Ninety dollars rent and fifty deposit."

"Deposit for what?"

"Damage."

Mark starts to say that there is nothing in the room worth that much, but he counts out the money and hands it to her when she cracks the door open. "No cooking in the room, and keep it quiet," she says as she hands him a receipt.

"Okay."

"Here's your key. Rent's due the first of every month."

By three, John is finished with eighteen holes, and feels ready to get home to Mark and Jean to try to make things right with them, to make them see that he didn't mean what he said and did last night, tell them that he is going for help. He parks his golf cart in the pro shop garage for recharging, thinks about going to the clubhouse for a drink, but no, no telling how long he would be there, get to drinking with some of the guys, maybe, and be there half the night. He can't bear the thought of once again fogging over his mind, wants now, needs, to keep what clarity has come upon him today. He must sustain these hopes that he can get over this business about the accident, and once again get along with his life.

The house is empty when John gets there, and he busies himself with putting the rest of Mark's belongings away and trying to fix the stereo turntable. He has it torn apart on the kitchen table when Jean gets home. There is a look of surprise on her face, and he connects it to the events of last night and sees only fear.

"Jean." She stands eyeing him warily. "I can't go on like I have been lately."

She drops her purse and books on the counter. "I can't either."

"I know. I'm sorry about last night. In the morning I'm going in the hospital."

"The hospital?"

"Dr. Branscom wants to run some tests. And he's going to start me on some sort of nerve medicine. Then

I'll go from there. No more drinking." She has turned away from him, but he continues. "I've been destroying our marriage. And Mark. I haven't been fair to him."

She turns to face him. "And what if you can't quit drinking? Do you think I'm going to go through any more of this hell you've made around here?"

"You're my wife." He looks at her, sees the statement has no impact, then looks down at the tile floor. "I'll join Alcoholics Anonymous. I'm quitting drinking. You don't have to believe me now. I'll show you."

Jean goes to the refrigerator and takes out the chicken breasts that will be their dinner. "Jean, are you even listening?"

"I've heard every word."

"Will you help me?" He's growing agitated, her disinterest hurting him.

"You're my husband. Of course I'll help. But things can't continue as they have."

"That's fair. If I can't get over," he starts to say the accident, and momentarily pictures the crumpled green car lying at the base of the rocky hillside, "over things, I'll leave. You can have everything here, and I'll leave. I want things to be like they used to be. We've had a lot of good years, haven't we?"

"We have." She looks into his troubled eyes now, realizing the truth of what he has said. She leans against the counter. "Will you quit this stuff about Jerry and me?"

"It's the drinking. I know there's nothing there. It just keeps coming out when I'm drinking. And I don't even know why." He takes the last step and pulls her to him and hugs her tightly, resting his head beside hers, cheeks touching. She puts her arms loosely around him and stares at the turntable parts spread over the table.

John is clearing the kitchen table when Mark walks in. He stops his work and looks sheepishly at Mark, who says hello and tries to walk on through the kitchen. But John heads him off at the doorway. Mark stands uncertainly, waiting for whatever it is John wants from him now.

"I'm sorry, Mark. Last night...I had no right. I don't expect you to forgive me, maybe not now anyways."

Mark shrugs. "We all do things we're sorry for, I guess. It's no big deal."

He slips past John and goes to his room. John looks blankly at Jean, who gives him a what-did-you-expect look. In a couple of minutes Mark comes back through the kitchen with a duffel bag. "Where are you going?"

"Got a room uptown."

"How are you going to live?" John asks.

"Found a job today."

"Doing what?"

"Pumping gas. Down at Walt's station."

John groans. "You can do better than that."

"I had a decent job, if you recall."

John nods slowly.

"Will you at least have dinner with us?" Jean asks.

John sees his chance. "Your car's fixed. All that was the matter was a punctured radiator. Had it fixed, pounded out the fender."

"Yeah?" The car is his; he bought it with the money he earned through the summer.

"Eat dinner with us, and I'll take you out to get it." There is pleading in his voice, and Mark starts out the door, then turns and drops his suitcase to the floor.

"Okay. I'll need wheels."

Waiting for dinner, Mark busies himself packing the rest of his things. After a few minutes John comes to his room. "You can stay here, you know."

Mark looks at him. "No, I don't think I can. Not anymore."

"Because of last night?"

"No. That's not really the reason. What were you doing when you were my age?"

The question catches John off guard, and he frowns to remember who he was at age twenty and what he was doing. "I was going to college, about the same as you were."

"You were a man, though, weren't you?"

After a moment John says, "Yes, I think I was, but things are different now. I made it so you could make it."

"Make what?"

John stands perplexed. "Make it...easier than I had to do it."

"You think I can't make it on my own?"

"No. Hell, no. I don't think that. You can do anything."

"Okay." He turns and resumes his packing, and John tries to think of something to say. But there is nothing.

Later, his car loaded with his belongings and dusk already coming on, bringing with it a hint of a cool evening, crisp like before the first frost, Mark leaves John and Jean sitting at the kitchen table. Jean has a sudden thought of Higby and is excited by it, but damns the thought for coming now, and she feels guilty as she watches Mark walk out of her life. She glances at John, haggard and red-faced from his recent binges of drinking and late hours. She sighs loudly, not so sure of anything anymore. Her many choices and options, her hopes and dreams, are nothing but confusion.

Chapter 22

"Want a beer?" Mark is coming out of his room after carrying the first load up the stairs, and is surprised. A short, stocky guy wearing a black t-shirt stands in the hallway holding a can of beer. Mark wonders how a little guy could have such big arms.

"Yeah, thanks. Let me get the rest of my stuff out of the car."

"Next room down," the other says and turns away, walking with a bad limp.

A couple more loads and Mark is finished. Then he gets his stereo set up and wired. He can't play any records, but the receiver can pick up several good FM stations with the antenna. Then he heads down to the next room. The short guy is sitting in an easy chair of the same vintage as the one in Mark's room, and a taller man with a long black beard and hair down to his shoulders sits on the bed. Mark has seen him in the Grotto a few times, but has never talked to him. "Beer's in the fridge," the little guy tells him. And, sure enough, there is beer in the fridge, at least four cases of the stuff, leaving little room for the sandwich meat and cheese which are squeezed into one corner.

Mark returns to the room and stands until the man on the bed moves over to make room for him. He thinks for a moment that he should introduce himself, shake hands and all that, but doesn't. Mark takes half the beer down in several huge swallows, the way he is used to doing.

"So how'd you end up in this hole?"

"About all I could afford. Ought to keep the rain off

me."

"That's Tony there," he says and points to the tall guy on the bed. "Just in from Columbus a couple months ago. Lived in the big house for a few years."

Mark turns and looks at him and nods. "Glad to meet you," he says and Tony nods back.

"I'm Merle," the little guy says.

"Mark's my name." Merle leans over to the table to change stations on the transistor radio.

"You guys want to listen to tunes, I've got a decent set-up. It'll pull YQ out of Columbus."

"All right." Tony says. "Used to listen to that in the pen. Guy next door had a stereo, kept it turned up for everybody to hear." Tony is first out the door, and Mark and Merle follow. "Decent," Tony says as he looks over Mark's stereo equipment. "Be right back," he says then.

"Get some more beer while you're out there," Merle calls after him. "Trying like hell to stay straight," Merle tells Mark about Tony. "Can't find a job, though, and if his P.O. catches him drinking or smoking dope he could go back in. You work?"

"Start a new job tomorrow. Pumping gas."

Merle laughs. "Shit, I'll bet my welfare pays more than that. What they paying you?"

"Two-twenty-five an hour."

Merle laughs. "I get a hundred twenty a week from the good old government."

Mark is surprised. Never thought about welfare, never knew anyone on it. "How do you manage that?"

Merle lifts his leg and slaps his foot. "Only got half a foot. Left part of it in Vietnam."

Mark nods solemnly as Tony steps back into the room and lights a joint. Merle turns up the volume as they pass it around.

"Doesn't the old lady downstairs care about the noise?" Mark asks.

"Turns her hearing aid off about now."

Merle pops the tab on his beer and takes the joint that Mark hands him. "Good system," Tony says to Mark.

"Fuck's all the noise?" comes a gruff voice from the doorway.

"Charlie, old buddy. Come on in," Merle tells the skinny old man standing there.

"Want a hit?" Tony asks him, holding the joint toward him.

"Hell, no. Smoke that chickenshit stuff. Shiiit."

"Well, then, get a beer, you old drunk."

"Guy's wasted. Liquor's got him, just riding it out."

It's good dope, and Mark gets off on it, but is starting to feel uncomfortable. Quite a group. He really hadn't thought about meeting anybody here, and is tired. The music is just loud enough that no one attempts to talk. Merle slumps back in the chair and closes his eyes. Tony sits staring ahead, eyes glued to the picture on the far wall. Mark sees it for the first time now. Strange he didn't notice it before. A grayish landscape of desert, somewhere in the western badlands, probably, backdrops a cowboy in leather vest and wrinkled hat, feet in the stirrups, head slumped over. Asleep in the saddle. The horse's head barely clears the ground, and his foreleg is dragging in the sand as he plods onward. Man and horse moving slowly forward, tired as hell, but can't or won't stop. Maybe they've got to be somewhere. More likely, Mark thinks, there is no place to stop that would be better than continuing on the way they are.

Just after eleven a girl wearing a green uniform stands in the doorway staring at them. "C'mon in," Tony says, the only thing he has said for better than an hour.

"This is Mark."

She nods to him as Tony names her: "Carla."

"Nice to meet you. Just get off work?" he asks.

"Yeah. Cleaned up after some old man all night.

"Work at the hospital?"

"Yeah."

In a couple of minutes she and Tony leave, and Mark turns the stereo down. Merle has dozed off, and Mark shakes him. Merle jumps to his feet, his bad foot buckling under, but he still manages to land a cross cut to Mark's stomach. Then Mark is on the floor, the wind knocked from him. "I'm sorry," Merle is saying as he helps Mark to his feet. "Are you all right?"

Mark stands gasping for air until he can talk. "Yeah. You always do that when somebody wakes you up?"

"I guess I was dreaming or something. Can't remember what it was though. I get a little hyper sometimes. Thanks for the tunes, man," he says, and limps away.

Mark turns off the receiver and takes another look around the room that is to be his home. He's tired, but lies for what seems a long time, listening to the sounds that old houses make in the night: the creakings and shiftings, occasional thumps. He hears the refrigerator open and close a couple of times, and very late, after he has been asleep for a while, hears Charlie come up the stairway and walk down the creaky-board hallway to his room.

The morning breaks dull and gray, the clouds that only threatened yesterday moved in for good now, solid gray banks of them lining the sky, a cold rain falling. John and Jean have breakfast together, but have little to say, even though John tries to talk to her. She is distant, will hardly look at him, and this is hard for John to take. Finally growing agitated, he asks her what is the matter. She says she has a headache, but he doesn't buy it. Even as rotten and out of control as he's been lately, he expects better from his wife. He's going to begin work on solving his problems today; the least she could do would be to give him a little support. "Look at me!" he finally says, the anger welling up in him.

She stares passively at him.

"You don't give a damn one way or the other, do you?"

"Too much has happened lately."

"I know that. But you're sitting there acting like I don't even exist. What's with you?"

"I'm tired of it, John. I don't really know what I want."

"Tired of what?"

She throws her hands into the air. "Everything. You. Us. You're not happy anymore."

"We agreed yesterday if I can't get out of whatever it is working on me, you can have your divorce, or whatever you want."

She looks quickly to him. Divorce is a big word for her, but was in her thoughts when John spoke it. "That's what we decided."

John is packing his suitcase when she leaves for school. She kisses him and says she'll come to see him at the hospital.

By one, John has been admitted and is in bed, relaxed from the Valium that the doctor ordered for him to have three times a day. He hasn't felt this calm for weeks, and the tension and strain of late gradually dissolve into drowsiness and he sleeps.

When he wakes in the early evening, John is hungry and watches as dinner trays on stainless steel carts are wheeled past his room. His roommate, installed while John was sleeping, sits on the edge of his bed eating. John raises his bed with the electric control, and the other man turns to look at him. He is about John's age, with hair that was once blond, turned now to a mottled gray.

"Must be nice," John says.

"What's that?"

"Getting to eat. I don't get anything tonight. Going to flush out the old system."

The other nods and turns back to his supper. But John feels like talking. "You from Oakridge?"

"Yeah."

"Work here?"

"Yeah. Been at Blatt Metal Works for twenty-one years."

"That's where I work, too!"

"Thought you looked familiar," the other says and turns again to look at John.

"I've been there almost as long as you have. Strange I never saw you."

"Welder. Hard to see anybody through a quarter inch of smoked glass."

"Yeah," John says, feeling the limitations that one or the other of them has. "What you in for?"

"Lung cancer." The other man doesn't turn around

again, and John looks at his back for many long moments before turning on the television with the remote control switch.

"Don't you have any rain gear?" Walt asks Mark as they stand in the cold drizzle by the gas pumps.

"No. I better get some, I guess, huh?"

Walt doesn't answer as the next car pulls ahead. "How're you today, Mr. Carver?" Walt calls as he turns the switch and plugs the nozzle in.

"Good. Check the brake fluid, would you, Walt? Pedal's a little spongy."

Mark stands watching, the cold rain trickling from his hair down his cheeks, as Walt pops open the master cylinder lid. "Little low," Walt says, and tells Mark where to get the brake fluid. In a few minutes, Mr. Carver on his way, Mark takes over with the next customer. "Fill it up for you?" he asks, as Walt instructed him to ask of everyone who drives up.

"Regular." Mark sets the pump on automatic and hurries around to the hood. His hands feel raw from the rain and cold steel of the pump. Rain gear. What a dummy. Should have gone out to K-Mart and gotten something before he came in. Never thought about it. When Walt leaves at five-thirty, he gives Mark his yellow rain slicker. He gives the roll of money to the other employee, who came in at five.

By quitting time, Mark's hands are red and puffy, and he helps Clint, a school teacher from Greenburg moonlighting to make a living, wheel in the oil racks, get the air hoses, battery fillers, and window squeegees from the pumps. Finally the day is over. On the way home Mark stops and buys a twelve pack. Might as well contribute to the beer supply in the refrigerator. When he gets there, he is surprised to find the door to his room open and Merle sitting in the easy chair wearing the stereo headphones. At least he's not asleep, Mark thinks, as he asks Merle how he got in the room. Merle slips the headphones off. "What?"

"How'd you get in here?"

"Same key fits all the doors. Didn't think you'd mind." Merle flicks a switch and pulls the cord out of the jack, and the music floods the room.

Mark rips open the twelve pack carton and hands a beer to Merle, who nods acceptance. About one o'clock, half the beer gone, Mark tells Merle he's tired. "Oh yeah, sure. Working man."

Mark falls asleep at once but wakes a couple hours later to a deep-throated coughing coming from the hall. Just Charlie trying to hack up his guts, the mincemeat inside that the cigarettes and booze have made through the years.

The next few days are cold and cloudy, with icy rain occasionally slashing down—gloomy, premature winter. Mark is settling into his new routine, learning the few things he needs to know at the station, getting to know the people in his house a little better. Thursday he gets stoned before he goes to work and finds that it is eight o'clock quickly, the busy time at the station past, and he and Clint sit and watch traffic.

John gets out of the hospital Thursday, having found that there is nothing wrong with him physically except the ulcer, and the doctor agrees to let him stay on the

Valium after John promises he won't drink while taking it. He is feeling better, relaxed from the medicine, but senses that night that Jean is removed from him somehow, but can't be sure, can't know whether it is something within him or if it's her. At least there is not the bitterness and arguing that have been with them lately, just this distance, as if they are waiting to see what will happen next, both wondering if divorce is a solution to their difficulties.

He has isolation and time Friday to think. One thing he realizes and is sure of is that he loves Jean. He knows, tries to imagine living without her, and it is inconceivable, and he is sure that she feels the same, deep down. But he also knows that he is going to have to make some major changes in himself and in the way he treats Jean and Mark. It will take time, but he knows he can change. And he is going to tell Jean how he feels, get a confirmation of love from her and go only forward, no more dwelling on what has happened. Hell, he's got it made, the house paid for, a beautiful wife, and Mark is ready to make his own way. And he'll also find a way to make things right with Elly Baker, somehow get her the money that will help her along.

Before Jean is home from school—said she had to go to the library for a while after class—John calls Mark at the station. "How's the job going?" he asks.

"Pretty good," Mark says. And the room? Good place to stay. Eating good? Sure. Pizza, burgers, chicken from the Colonel Sanders drive-in next to the gas station.

"Do you know where Elly Baker is now?"

"Staying with Frank till she has the baby."

"Okay," John says, having found out what he wanted to know. He'll go to the bank in the morning and have a check drawn from his account, drop it in the mail, and that will be that. When Jean gets home at five-thirty, John has the evening all planned out—they'll go out to dinner, maybe catch a movie or go bowling, anything to have fun together like they used to. Just be together, tell her at the right time how he feels. He is excited as she goes about getting dressed, feels the old energy returning, feels good, worries gone now that he has made these positive decisions today.

They go to the club to eat and get a table in the corner where they are alone. John has coffee while Jean has a drink before they are served their steaks. She is quiet, sipping slowly on her collins, looking around the room to see who is here tonight, waving occasionally at other couples, smiling at them in her charming way. She turns back to John and catches him staring at her, a smile on his face.

She doesn't look away, and he keeps smiling, staring, until she laughs out of nervousness and curiosity. "What is it?" she asks him.

"You. You're very beautiful."

"Hmmm." But she is flattered. Higby hinted earlier in the week that she was fairly well preserved, but hadn't told her she was beautiful, or even pretty. What was it he had said? "You're okay, babe." Babe. That was the part that got her. And she laughs as she thinks of it: Babe.

John reaches across the table and takes her hand, and she lets him hold it. "I love you very much, Jean." He sees the surprise, concern, or whatever it is on her face, but goes on. "I haven't told you that for a long time, but I need to tell you. I love you."

She stares across the table at him, tries with the faintest pressure to disengage her hand from his, but he holds tightly and doesn't seem to notice. "What if we were to have our own private little wedding, you know, make up some vows of our own and reaffirm the good things we have, all the good that we have left for us?"

She swallows hard and pulls her hand firmly away now. "That's silly. Why would you want to do that?"

"To reaffirm the good things we've felt and said to each other through the years."

"I don't know." She looks around the room as if expecting someone to be eavesdropping on their conversation, but the nearest couple is engaged in talk, and she looks back to John.

John is hurt by her hesitation. In a few moments he asks, "If I asked you to marry me again, would you?"

"We can't talk about this now. It's just not the right time."

"You can't say you love me? Or want me as your husband anymore?"

"I can't say it for sure right now. I need some time, John."

"Time?"

"A few weeks. A month. I want to be able to make the commitment you're asking for."

"But we made the commitment over twenty years ago, in a church, before God."

They are silent as the waiter brings the sizzling steaks to their table. They have the food to take up the slack now, and in a few minutes Doc Marley and his wife are sitting at the table next to them and there are the pleasantries to be exchanged, talk of the tidbits of their lives that they share with acquaintances at the club.

By the time they are back home, John has regained his enthusiasm and energy and makes plans for the next day: he needs to buy new weather-stripping for the doorsills, and paint for the laundry room in the basement, a chore he has put off since building the house. Dr. Branscom told him to stay busy so he wouldn't drink, and John intends to follow the advice.

He makes love to Jean later, and knows she loves him. If she can't say it now, she will in a week or so. She can have her time. He can wait.

John is up early, the calming Valium somehow giving him back his usual energy and enthusiasm. He cooks pancakes for breakfast and wakes Jean when they are ready. She is surprised and amused, but it really is a treat for her to get up to a breakfast already cooked, the coffee steaming at her place at the table. John talks excitedly of his plans for the day. If he gets tired of painting, he can always cut firewood from the maple the electric company cut down behind the house.

Exactly at nine o'clock he is on his way to the Oakridge Hardware Store for the paint and weather-stripping, and after that he intends to go to the bank. He feels good, strong again, happy.

Jean realizes as she clears the table that John is really trying, and when she thinks of Higby and her writing feels a distressing pang of guilt. Has she been wrong in going forward with her life, trying to grow in new directions? No, she thinks not. She would do it all over again, would change nothing of the new feelings of accomplishment and intrigue that her attempts at writing and her relationship with Higby have provided her. She thinks of Jerry and on an impulse dials the number at the newspaper.

"Jerry, this is Jean. How are you?"

"I'm fine. How about yourself?"

"Great. Things are going real well."

"How's John doing? I heard he was in the hospital."

"Oh, he's fine. Changed a lot this week. He finally admitted to himself that he has a problem."

"Damn," John says to himself and thumps the steering wheel with the palm of his hand. Forgot to measure the weather-stripping for the doors. He wheels into a driveway, turns around and heads back home. Just before he turns onto his street he sees Millie Blatt ahead of him. He honks the horn, and she waves as she sees him in the rearview mirror. At home, he hurries into the kitchen to get his wood rule to measure the stripping.

He stands over the drawer where he keeps his few household tools, and when he finds the rule, glances at Jean. "Who you talking to?" he asks, and has already turned away from her to get on with his work when she answers, "Millie."

He stops. Millie? How could that be? Millie couldn't have gotten to a phone since he saw her a minute ago. He goes to the door and sets the rule on the floor. Jean is talking away to Millie, saying something now about whether she and Bill are going to the cocktail party at the Wilson's. She is ready to say good-bye when John moves across the room and crowds close to the phone. But she covers the receiver and tells him, "Get away."

He gets away, yeah, he'll get away all right. His hands are shaking as he extends the rule joint by joint. Jean hangs up the phone. "What's Millie up to this morning?" he asks, trying to remain calm.

"Going shopping. You know, the usual."

He approaches her, rigid with his knowledge of her

untruth. It had to be a man. "You liar. Who were you talking to?"

Jean looks blankly and fearfully to him and turns and walks into the living room. He follows, restraining himself as best he can. She sits on the couch looking down at the thick carpet beneath her slippers.

"It was a man, wasn't it? You're going to tell me who you were talking to." He paces back and forth, the flowing adrenalin making him unconscious of his actions. He stops and stands over her, starts to reach for her, but restrains himself. She looks slowly up to him. "You wouldn't understand. 1 can't tell you now."

"Like hell."

She sees how he is when she looks at him, the anger and hurt etched over his face. "I was talking to Jerry."

He paces the floor again. "Jerry. You and Jerry. All this time I was right. You and Jerry," he keeps muttering as he walks quickly back and forth.

"It's not what you think."

"You had to lie to me when you're talking to my best friend?"

"I knew you wouldn't understand. We're just friends, and the way you've been lately I couldn't tell you who it was."

"I ought to," he says, but stops. He can't touch her, unfaithful but still precious to him.

John is barely conscious of driving, but in a few minutes he is at the newspaper office. "Where's Jerry?" he demands of the receptionist.

"I believe he's on the phone right now," she says and glances at the small switchboard before her. "Oh, there, the light just went out. I'll see if he's busy now."

John is in Jerry's office before she can dial his

extension. He stands up as John enters. "John. Come on in."

John walks slowly toward the desk. "Just get off the phone?"

"Yeah. Been a busy morning."

"How long have we known each other?" John asks, seeking his eyes, but Jerry looks down. "How long?"

"Nineteen, twenty years."

"You and Jean. How could you?"

"There's nothing there, John." Jerry meets John's gaze now. "Nothing," he says quietly. Jean called him while John was on his way to the office. If only she hadn't dragged him into her deception about the phone call, an unnecessary deception at that.

"You don't lie about nothing." The rage flares again as John thinks of Jerry sitting here going along with Jean's lie.

"You don't understand, John." Jerry thinks of what Jean told him last week about her seeing another man.

John stands before the desk. It would be easy to reach across and grab him by the throat and jerk him across the desk, throw him into the wood-paneled wall, using all the pumped-up energy he is trying to keep under control. "We've known each other a long time. Long time," John says and walks out.

John backs out of the parking space in the asphalt parking lot, jams the shifter into drive and tromps the accelerator to the floor. He is satisfied by the angry squeal of the tires, glad for the power in this machine. As he turns onto the street, he squeals the tires again and drives with a satisfied smirk on his face. Make a good news story: John Holz, prominent citizen, arrested for reckless operation, him and the usual bunch of hot-rodders. Also arrested for DWV—Driving While Valiumized. He reaches in his shirt pocket for the small pill bottle he carries everywhere now and takes another ten milligrams of the calming stuff. Or maybe DWA—Driving While Angry.

But the amusing and ridiculous thoughts disappear. Where can he go now, what can stop the terrible ache inside? No wonder Jean has been acting the way she has—going out with his best friend, of all people. Why couldn't she have picked somebody else? Now he is going to lose not only his wife but Jerry, the one person he could have gone to for talk or reassurance right now.

He parks on the square and sits in front of the hotel. What the hell, he finally thinks, man was not meant to cope with things such as this without the aid of alcohol.

The bar is deserted, and John looks at his watch, a little surprised. No wonder there's no one here. It's not even ten o'clock yet. But just as well; he doesn't feel like talking to anyone. He wonders if the place is even open as he sits on the bar stool looking at himself in the mirror behind the row of bottles. He brushes his hair to the side, turns this way and that studying his profile, and tries to smile through the glare stuck on his face. Twenty years, and the old lady gets hot pants for your best friend. Damn.

"Hi, John," the bartender calls as he comes out of the back room, a case of beer resting against his stomach. "Didn't know anybody was out here."

"You open yet, Ed?"

"Yeah, sure. What can I get you?"

"Double bourbon. Water chaser."

Ed pours the drink into a glass and tips the bottle up for an extra half shot. "How you been?" he asks John as he sets the liquor and water on the bar.

"Good. No, not good. Hell, I don't know," he says.

John downs the drink quickly, throws a couple dollars on the bar, and is on his way. The alcohol feels warm and good in his stomach as he drives home.

Jean is sitting in the kitchen. John walks past her, grabs a bottle of bourbon from the liquor cabinet, gets a juice glass out of a cupboard and sits down across from her. He pours a little of the stuff in the glass and throws it down, jerking his head back like the cowboys do on TV when they hit the saloon from a cattle drive.

"You're not supposed to drink," she says calmly.

"You're not supposed to screw my best friend either." He pours another one, but lets it set in front of him.

She shakes her head slowly back and forth. "You don't understand."

He's tired of hearing this morning that he doesn't "understand."

"What's to understand? You and Jerry had to lie to me so I wouldn't know what's been going on."

"But it's not the way it looks," she says, raising her voice a little in frustration.

That's all it takes. He points his finger at her. "You're a liar and a sneak."

"You're crazy," she says. "You're nuts."

He smiles a lopsided grin and rolls his eyes.

To hell with it, to hell with him and this mess that is her life with him. "All right," she says and storms out of the room. He can hear her banging around in the bedroom as she goes about packing her bags. And then it hits him. He's really losing her, already lost her. Twenty years. He gets up to go to her and try to reverse what has happened, take back what he said. But he stops in the living room, dizzy, and sits down in his chair. When she comes marching through the room, he watches her sadly. It happened too fast.

Jean sets her bags down in the kitchen and looks back. Quickly she opens a cupboard and takes one of their savings passbooks. She'll have money anyway. In the library she assembles the beginnings of her novel, and puts the folder of notes and outlines in the case with her typewriter.

The anger returns as John listens to the door slam behind her. What the hell is a man supposed to do when he catches his wife sneaking around with another man? His anger and hatred are pure and righteous.

Chapter 23

In a half hour Jean is standing before Higby's apartment. She knocks again, louder. He's got to be here. The door is slowly drawn open, and Higby stands before her in his bathrobe, blinking into the morning light.

"I was afraid you wouldn't be here."

"I'm here." He steps into the small kitchen and puts on the tea kettle. Jean stands in the foyer watching him. Finally he turns to face her.

"So, what's happening this morning?"

"All sorts of exciting things," she says, trying to keep her voice light. "It's not every day you decide to get a divorce."

"Because of us?" he asks, not savoring the thought of an irate husband seeking him out.

"No. It has nothing to do with us." He sits down, relieved. "He thinks I was involved with his best friend. It's all too silly to explain. He's just gotten paranoid in the past few weeks. He's crazy."

"You're certain you're getting a divorce?"

"It's certain as far as I'm concerned."

Higby doesn't want any part of anybody else's divorce; his own was bad enough. He knows how people act when they go about tearing apart and discarding the last five, ten, twenty years of their lives. He pictures himself breaking up the coffee table with a ball bat in his New York apartment after his wife filed for their divorce. Her trying to set fire to the manuscript he was working on then. He looks at Jean and shakes his head slowly back and forth.

"What's the matter?"

"Are you sure you know what you're getting into?"

"I'm sure of what I'm getting out of."

He laughs as the tea kettle whistles. "Want coffee?"

"Please." She sits looking around the apartment, listening to him open the jar, pour the water, hears the spoon chiming lightly against the edges of the cups.

"You wouldn't need a roommate, would you?" she asks as he sets the cups on the table.

He knew that was coming. "You want to make things hard on yourself?" he asks, trying to figure the best angle to dissuade her from wanting to move in with him.

"What do you mean?"

"The divorce. Once it's decided you're finished, you'll end up looking at the economic side of things. If your husband can prove you're living with another man, the judge will be on his side. You'll end up with nothing."

"I don't want anything he has," she says quickly, really believing what she is saying, and feels her purse, which contains the five hundred in cash and the four thousand dollar check from the savings account. "Okay, you're right. I can't move in here yet."

Yet? Higby shudders inwardly. She was there when he needed it, but he wonders now if it has been worth it. Better, perhaps, to stick with the go-go girls.

"So. 1 guess I'd better try to find an apartment today. Are there any open here?"

"I don't think so. But these aren't furnished or anything, just the stove and refrigerator."

She realizes she has no furniture. She could go back home and take some of the things from the house, but she doesn't want to see John again. "I'll need a furnished place, I guess. Do you have a newspaper?"

He reaches for last night's Cranston daily. "I guess I'd better get busy and find a place," she says and stands up. "What are you doing tonight?"

"Nothing special." Maybe he can keep on seeing her without getting involved.

"Want me to stop back this evening?"

"Yeah. Might as well. We can have a few drinks, maybe go out for a while. You don't know many people here in Cranston, do you?"

"A few from the country club. None of them very well." She tucks the newspaper under her arm and starts for the door, Higby behind her.

She kisses him and is on her way.

John sits in a daze in the spacious living room. He doesn't want to lose Jean. But there is also the other voice crying for revenge, telling him that he would have no pride if he found Jean and asked her to come back.

He sets the drink on the table beside his easy chair and looks at it suspiciously. Already he can feel the stuff taking control of him.

Outside, the cloud cover is mostly gone and the sun slants brilliantly through the woods behind the house. He picks up the glass, tosses off the rest of the drink and decides to go to the country club. Maybe he can find a game with somebody. And if he's going to drink, the last resort, he might as well do it in the company of high class alcoholics.

He sees a few players on the course as he drives down the winding asphalt road. Doesn't see any of his regular playing partners, though. He can play by himself if he has to.

John is a little dizzy from his early drinking and is well on his way to his worst round of golf in years by the fifth hole. After the sixth, he decides to give it up and runs his electric cart flat out across the deserted fairways. Might have been different if he'd had a game lined up. But he was planning to spend the day working around the house, and with Jean. What a sick feeling. So many things gone haywire all at once.

Even the country club bar is deserted. None of his drinking buddies there, just the bartender sitting at the counter reading a newspaper. Once there, John has lunch. He drinks a couple of beers with his hamburger and fries. When he leaves the club, he doesn't know where to go. He'd like to beat on somebody and thinks of Jerry and Jean. He had his chance for that this morning, but it would still be nice to get a stranglehold on one or the other of them and rattle their worthless brains a little. He goes back home and sits, restless but nothing to do, and takes another Valium.

Evening finds John in the kitchen looking dumbly at the nearly empty bottle of bourbon. He needs to relax, he thinks, and takes another Valium, the seventh one of the day. He thinks of the accident again, the scene coming clearly through the booze, and he sees it all happen again, though this time at a distance as an observer. He hears the steel crunching together, sees the car parts whizzing through the air, watches as the old green car smashes into the rocks. And the sirens and patrolmen. By God. The police. They should have hauled him off to jail for murder. That's what they should have done, but they didn't know the truth. Well, he'll fix that. His clumsy fingers plod through the telephone book. It takes him several minutes to find the listing for the Highway Patrol in Cranston. On the second try he rings the right number.

"Highway Patrol," the officer says.

"Sis plish?"

"What?"

"Sis plish?"

"Yeah. Yeah, Highway Patrol."

"I killt a man."

"When did this happen?"

"Oh, month, weeks before."

"Before what."

"For she lef."

"How did it happen?" the cop asks John.

"Crashed him in a wall."

"Listen, what did you say your name was?"

"John Holds."

"And who did you kill?"

"Uke Baer."

"Listen, Mr. Holds, why don't you just go to sleep and call it a day?"

"I gilled im. Damnit. I'm a murderr."

"Okay," the cop says as another call comes in. "Tell you what. You get a good night's sleep and call the police in the morning, and they can get in touch with us."

Finally John gets the phone back on its wall hook. They don't even believe him. He'll go to sleep, all right, he thinks. He takes out his pill bottle and tries to count out three pills, but doesn't know how many he puts in his mouth and washes down with the last couple ounces of bourbon. He gets up and staggers into the living room, where he lies down in the middle of the plush gold carpet.

Things back to normal, the speed coursing through the system, the strong stuff convincing the mind that it is meant to exist for this moment only. Drinking beer after beer. Laughing as Frank tells his joke to Merle and Tony, and Old Charlie, coaxed into the party by a can of beer.

"So what we going to do?" Mark asks, more to Frank than to the others, but all are included if they want to be. Tony looks at his watch. "I told Carla I'd see her after work."

"That's all right," Frank clowns. "You go ahead with the boys and have a good time. I'll look after her for you."

Tony laughs. "That's nice of you."

They pile out of the room, knowing it's time to go somewhere. Charlie sneaks down the stairs while Merle and Frank and Mark talk about where they're going. Charlie knows where to go—down to the Corner Cafe. His buddies will be there, guys buying him drinks all night.

Merle tells them about a place in Cranston where you can get a good meal, steak or whatever you want, for around seven dollars. That's all they need to hear, and in a minute are piled into the front seat of Frank's truck, headed for Cranston. They smoke a number on the way and are good and primed for the feed when they reach the Trapper's Inn.

The place looks too small to hold the number of people represented by the many cars in the gravel parking lot. Merle limps along ahead of them, and soon they are seated at a table, and Frank is eating one of the hard rolls left in the basket as the waitress begins clearing the table. Beads of sweat stand on her forehead. She doesn't look at the three characters seated there. "Long night?" Frank asks. She rolls her eyes. "Just getting started."

"Tell you what," Frank says. "You get us a pitcher of beer and don't worry about ordering up our grub till you're good and ready."

She looks at him and smiles as she dumps the rest of the dishes into the plastic tub. "You're a doll," she says and hustles the tub back into the kitchen. In a minute she is back with a pitcher and three glasses. Mark wonders how he does it, how Frank can make a roomful of people laugh and forget everything, how he can understand the feelings of so many people, different kinds of people, why people like him, laugh with him, smile, love or hate him. Some do hate him, just as many as like him. But they all know for sure one way or the other. Up front, no fakery, maybe that's it.

The beer is going down good tonight, and Merle is opening up a little, talking about himself like he hasn't done before, and Mark listens intently as he talks about his folks, who live here in Cranston, as he tells about the night he lost his foot, wading waist-deep through a swamp. The water saved his life, muffled the blast— could have lost more than the foot. They drink and talk, and about the time the pitcher needs refilling, the waitress is back. "Thanks for waiting," she says to Frank, and they order steaks and potatoes and another pitcher of beer.

Later, as they sit laughing and talking, content with

the good meal, Mark sees a bearded man holding the door for a woman. All he sees is her back, but he is sure it's his mother.

Nothing else planned for the night, they have another pitcher of beer, and Frank gets the waitress's phone number. Soon they are back in Frank's truck. When they near Oakridge a short time later, Mark asks Frank if he'll stop by his folks' house so he can get his watch and a couple other things. Now would be a good time. He can say his friends are waiting, and he has to go right away. They would want him to sit and visit and talk. And he's invulnerable to anything they might say or do. "Sure thing," Frank says, and in a few minutes they are at the Holz home.

Mark sees only one light on in the house. "They're not even home," he says. "I'll get my watch." Frank pulls alongside the kitchen door, the sound of the old flathead ricocheting off the house in a healthy purr. Mark finds his watch on the kitchen counter. As he slips it on, he looks into the living room.

"Dude's got money, hey?" Merle asks Frank.

"Yeah. His folks do," Frank says and tunes in a different radio station. Then Mark is at the door. "Help me!" he shouts. "Come on!" Mark darts back into the house, Frank and Merle right behind him. They find Mark kneeling over John in the living room.

"Just drunk?" Frank asks. Merle stands casing the place. Never can tell, might come in handy some time.

"No," Mark says, holding John's wrist, feeling for the pulse. "Can't wake him up. Call an ambulance," Mark tells Frank. "Must have had a heart attack or something."

They wait after Frank calls, Frank and Merle

kneeling on the floor beside Mark, who holds his father's wrist. Pulse only about thirty a minute. "You know mouth to mouth?"

"Yeah," Frank says. Merle knows it, too, and more. "If the heart stops, let me know," he tells Mark. "Took a course on heart attacks, pulmonary something or other."

In a few minutes they can hear the siren of the approaching ambulance, and Frank goes out to motion it into the driveway. The van speeds up the drive, its red light slashing through the darkness. On the way back through the kitchen, Frank sees the pill bottle on the oak table, small blue tablets lying scattered around it. He looks at the prescription and takes it into the living room. The attendants have John on the stretcher, and one of them is taking his pulse and blood pressure. "Here," Frank says, and hands the bottle to the other.

"Overdose," he tells his partner, and they waste no more time checking vital signs. They stow the stretcher and body into the back of the van. "Up front," one of them tells Mark, and in a moment he sits looking into the lighted rear of the van as they speed toward the hospital, the driver on the radio to the emergency room.

"I guess we should lock the place up," Frank says as he and Merle stand beside the truck.

"Yeah," Merle says. "Hey, what was the dope?"

"Valium. Tens."

Merle goes back into the house and gathers the pills off the table into the palm of his hand. "Hard to come by," he explains a few moments later as Frank checks to make sure the door is locked.

"Fucking vulture."

"Hey. They ain't going to do him any good."

Mark sits on the white plastic chair in the waiting

room, smoking a cigarette he bummed off the other man there. Nearly an hour has passed when Mark is snubbing out his third cigarette. A nurse appears in the doorway and looks in. "Holz?"

Mark jumps up. "Is he all right?"

"He should pull through."

The clickety-clacking of the typewriter seems far away as Mark gives his father's address and employer for   the   insurance   forms.

Chapter 24

Waking up but not really awake. Feels a pain in his arm, something plugged in his nose. His throat, chest and stomach hurting. Tries to move, hasn't the strength. Where is he? Then he feels it coming, can't stop it. He tries to sit up and moves just enough to attract the attention of one of the nurses. She looms over him, fuzzy and out of focus for some reason, but he sees her white uniform and realizes he is in the hospital.

He hears her call to someone. They work his gown off him, telling him to lie still, and his own stench comes to him as they unpin what looks like a diaper and go about cleaning him up. The water is warm and feels good. Then one of them holds his legs up while the other slips another diaper under him. Was he in a wreck? Why is he in the hospital? he tries to ask, but his words are unclear. One of the nurses leans over him. He can smell her perfume, and is glad for it as it replaces the stench momentarily. "You're in intensive care," he hears her say. "You took too much of your medicine." Medicine? What medicine? He hasn't been sick for years. Not John Holz. "The doctor will be here this afternoon to see you. You're going to be all right."

All right? Lying here helpless wearing diapers, not even sure this is real? Then the fog rolls in, and he is asleep again.

"French toast!" Higby says as he enters the kitchenette. "Haven't had this for years."

"I always fix it on Sunday mornings," she says, pouring the hot water for instant coffee. She thinks of John momentarily. French toast on Sundays. A habit, behavior resulting from twenty years together. How many of these little habits will she keep? It doesn't matter, she realizes, as she sits down across from Higby. Now is what is important.

"You're all right," he tells her, and smiles. "Haven't had anyone fix me breakfast. for a long time. Don't even bother to eat it anymore."

"Was your wife a good cook?"

Higby looks up, surprised, swallows and considers. "No," he finally says. "She wasn't much interested in cooking. It always made me angry. She didn't work, well, a couple of days a week at this art gallery one of her friends owned, and she couldn't even get it together to fix me a decent meal."

Jean listens intently. She is good at being a housewife. But how could Higby set much store by these outdated values, how could he value cooking and housecleaning over creativity and intellect in a wife? "You're a chauvinist," she states flatly.

He shrugs. "Look around. It's still mostly the man who gets out and earns the money to live on. Lots of women aren't working for the money. Call it fulfillment or some such baloney."

"You can't really mean that. Lots of women make good money, and if the rest don't, it's because they haven't had the same opportunities that men have had."

"Peace," Higby says.

"Okay. But you mean that if you were ever to be married again, your wife would be the cook? Like a maid?"

He smiles and nods. "Great breakfast!"

"I can't believe you're saying these things. What about companionship? Trust? Faith in each other?"

"You're the one that's married. How about it? Did it work? Any of that stuff keep your marriage together?"

Jean gasps. "You're worse than a chauvinist."

Higby laughs. He's feeling good today. "Peace," he says again, seeing that she's taking it wrong. "I don't mean all of that." She laughs then, realizing he's been putting her on. But she thinks of John again. How easy it would be to go home to him and try to make up. But no. She has this other life now. Maybe if he hunts her down and begs her to come back....

Higby looks at his watch as he mops up the leftover maple syrup with the last bit of toast. "Got to get to work pretty quick."

They have a second cup of coffee together, talk a little about her book and the one he is working on, and it's already afternoon. When Jean is ready to leave, after washing the dishes, she tells him she'll let him know where she'll be living.

"Okay. Yeah, let me know," he says as he closes the door behind her. He told her he was busy tonight, had a meeting at the school to go to.

At one-thirty Mark finally gets a message that he can see his father. John is awake now, still hooked up to the intravenous fluid, but they have taken the oxygen hose off and lifted the back of the bed so he can sit up. Mark barely recognizes him the way his face is all puffy and red, big black bags under his blood-red eyes. Mark leans over and kisses John's cheek, the first he has kissed him since he was what?—ten years old or thereabouts? He pulls away quickly as he feels the rough stubble.

"How you feeling?"

It is still hard for John to talk, but he manages to say terrible. Mark nods and sits down on the chair beside the bed. He looks around the room, sees other patients lying wired up like John, hooked into cardiograph machines, heartbeats showing up like on the electronic tennis game they hook to the TV set at home.

"How'd I get here?"

"You drank too much and took too much of your medicine."

John still doesn't remember any medicine at home. The last thing he remembers is playing golf. But what day or with whom he can't place.

Mark talks so John doesn't have to, talks about his job and his room and the new friends he has made, tries to paint a rosy picture of his life for John so at least John won't worry about him anymore. But John lies confused, trying to make sense of what Mark is saying, and none of it fits together for him. Then the nurse tells Mark he has to go. Mark stands up, takes John's hand in his, sees how weak he is, and leans over and kisses him again. So close to dying. So close and Mark hasn't kissed him for years.

When Branscom comes to see John on Monday, he has a plan worked out. He has already called Doctor Williams, the Cranston psychiatrist to whom he refers his patients in need of counseling. He knows he couldn't just turn John loose again. Even if he is only drinking, no Valium or anything to go with it, the man is obviously sick.

John is clearer-minded this morning, but still his memory is fuzzy. Little snatches of things keep coming back to him. He remembers playing golf Saturday morning. He remembers the phone call and Jean's departure. But other things of his past keep coming to him as if they happened Saturday, and he is confused and frustrated.

Branscom gets down to business right away. "You nearly killed yourself," he tells John. "And it would have been partly my fault for trusting you to take your medication as I prescribed it."

John nods his swollen face. "It was because...."

"I don't want to hear 'because' anything. I'm referring you to a psychiatrist in Cranston. I've arranged for you to be admitted to the psychiatric ward this afternoon."

John sits up in alarm. What? Him in the nut house? "No," he says quickly. "I'm not going there."

"You don't have any choice in the matter. If I need to, I'll have a judge draw up a court order admitting you. From what your son and your friend, Jerry Shunk, have told me, your wife left you, and I don't want you to be home by yourself."

"That bastard," John says. "He ought to know why she left me. He and she...."

"Save it," Branscom says. "You're angry, hurt, and weak from what you've done to yourself. Will you go along with the treatment in Cranston?"

John considers as Branscom stands up and gets ready to go. The psych ward? John Holz? Ah, but he's so tired. Maybe he could just lie there and sleep for a few days, talk to the psychiatrist and then get out. Better that way than have it get to a judge. "Can I leave there when I want?"

"If you sign yourself in, you'll have that choice after a week or so. But I think you should let your doctor there evaluate you. Then follow his advice. It's not a bad place. You're free to move around as you wish. There's a lounge. Most of the people are like you. They've reached a point in their lives which, for some reason, is too much to handle. Give it a try?" John nods assent, unable to talk because of the lump in his throat.

After lunch, John dozes off, and when he wakes, Mark is standing by his bed. "How you feeling?" Mark asks.

John looks away and stares at the blip representing an old man's fading heartbeat. He looks back to Mark. "You know where I'm going?"

Mark nods. "Dr. Branscom explained it to me. I brought some clothes for you," he says and lifts the paper bag he is holding at his side. "There's a suitcase in the car with the other things you'll need. You can wear regular clothes there."

There. A good name for the place.

John realizes how weak he really is when he gets out of the wheelchair in the lobby and walks the several yards to Mark's car. So tired. He asks Mark if he has seen Jean. Mark doesn't like telling him, but says "no." Branscom told him not to let John get to talking about his problems. Mark does explain on the way to Cranston that he talked to Bill Blatt and he'll be covered at the office, have his work kept up while he's in the hospital. But John doesn't care about his job. He just wants to get rid of these sick and hurt feelings. Be anything but what he is. He sits in silence the rest of the way to Cranston

General, and Mark turns the radio on to take up the slack.

They get through Admitting in a half hour, and as Mark walks behind his father and the skinny orderly, he begins to have his own doubts about John being here. They wait at the end of a corridor until a nurse unlocks the thick, glass doors and lets them on the ward. The hallways are carpeted. Chrome hand rails along the walls. A very tall man with huge, black circles under his eyes stands in the doorway to the lounge, watching them. Mark glimpses several people in the room before the television. He stops for a moment to watch two teenagers playing ping-pong.

Then they are in John's room. The place has a strange odor to it, like somebody was real sick there and the mess was cleaned up by spraying sterilizer and deodorant into the room. John sits quietly on the bed while Mark opens the suitcase and names off the belongings that John will have here with him. "People steal things here," the orderly laughs, when Mark asks him why he has to write down what everybody brings with them.

Mark sits in the chair beside the bed for a few minutes, finally sees that John wants to be alone, and asks him if there is anything else he needs. "You brought cigarettes, didn't you?"

"Two cartons."

When Mark turns and says, "See you later," John lifts a hand, staring down.

John sits listening, trying to accustom himself to the laughter and shouts coming from the lounge. From down the hall he hears a hoarse female voice calling, "Nurse. Nurse. Somebody." Concentrating on the voice, he sits trying to picture the woman, whomever she might be, and comes up with nothing. "Nuuurr- se, help me."

John lights a cigarette and looks out the window to the parking lot. The clouds and gloom of winter are back, and he watches the wind whip a windbreak of ginko trees that act as a barrier between a large stone house and the hospital lot. He inhales the smoke deeply and sits very still on the bed. When will he see this psychiatrist? he wonders. Today? He hopes so. Get this thing moving, do what he has to do and get the hell out. But then what? he asks himself. Get out and do what? Work. Play. Take a vacation, maybe. He has a week left this year, could catch a flight out of Columbus and go just about anywhere. He takes another drag from his cigarette, and there is a clanging in the hallway. Then the door to his room slams shut by itself. He gets up and puts out his cigarette. The clanging hasn't stopped, and John opens the door to the hallway.

"Stay in your room," a young girl dressed in white tells him as she rushes past. Other patients are milling around in the hallways, nurses, aides and orderlies trying to get them back to their rooms.

"What's going on?" John asks one of them.

"Fire." the other says. "The hospital's on fire." John stays in the hall with him, a skinny, stoop-shouldered man with one of his front teeth missing and the other stained yellow by nicotine.

In a few minutes the firemen come rushing onto the floor. They look strange here, with their thick black slickers, helmets shiny under the fluorescent lighting, a couple of them carrying fire extinguishers, others with long-handled heavy axes.

In a minute they have all gathered at the end of the

hallway by John's room. A couple of them come out of the room. "Just a cigarette," one of them says to a nurse. The patients are gathered around by now. Most look like they are visiting here, wearing their street clothes, talking to one another in their excitement. A few are different, though. A short boy with his head shaved stands behind most of the others reading from a Bible. A big man with long, greasy hair, clad in a hospital gown, sits strapped in a wheel chair. "Hah," he says angrily. "Who cares? It's just another day. Three hundred and sixty-five a year, whether you include Christmas or not. Mother Earth don't know the difference." A very fat woman is talking excitedly in a high shrill voice to one of the other patients. "Whose room is it?" she keeps asking. From down the hallway comes the voice calling, "Nuu-r-rse. Nuu-u-rrse." John leans against the wall. He feels someone crowd up to him and looks down to see a woman of about thirty-five staring up at him. She looks into his eyes, no expression on her face, and presses closer until John steps away from her.

"There he is," he hears someone say, and all eyes are on him. "You set off the smoke alarm," one of them tells him. He caused all this? A nurse takes him by the arm. He shakes it loose. What now? "I was just coming to see you," the woman explains to him calmly. "Let's go in your room."

The crowd breaks up with laughter and horseplay. The woman, her long, dark hair tied into a ponytail, tells John to sit on the bed as she takes the chair by the window. She hands him a paper. "Business first. I'm Mrs. Taylor, the floor coordinator. This gives you all the rules."

"No smoking in rooms" is the number one item on

the list. He scans the rest, unimportant little things like no visitation in other patients' rooms, no TV past eleven o'clock, visiting hours, et cetera. He puts the paper down, and she hands him another listing "The Psychiatric Patient's Bill of Rights." He looks quickly through this one, which simply tells him they can't do anything to him unless he understands it and has been informed of the possible complications of treatment.

When he looks up again she is smiling, and it makes him uncomfortable. "Well," she says, taking a paper out of a folder, "Would you mind answering a few questions for me?" Her voice is slow and warm, maybe a little on the syrupy side, but John says sure, fire away.

"Why do you think you're here?"

"Blackmail," John answers quickly.

"Blackmail?" She writes something on the paper and looks back to him. "How do you mean?"

"My doctor told me to be here or he'd take it to court."

She writes quickly. "But don't you think he was trying to do what was best for you?"

"I don't know."

"Why do you think he wanted you here?"

"I guess he was afraid I'd hurt myself." She seems really interested in him, and he feels more relaxed.

"Do you think you would hurt yourself if you were back home?"

"I might get drunk, but that's about all, I think."

"You were pretty sick for a couple of days."

John nods, making a sour face as he remembers.

"Not much fun?" Her voice is soft, compassionate.

"No. I guess I almost died."

"You don't want to die, do you?"

He laughs. Nobody has ever asked him such a silly question. "Does anybody?"

"I think most people have times when they feel they would be better off dead than alive." John nods as her statement sinks in. "What things have happened lately that caused you to end up here?"

John looks at her, the confusion evident on his face.

"I mean, are there any things that have happened lately that have made you want to drink, or that have caused you to worry?" The confusion deepens.

"Nothing?" she asks, prodding him onward.

"A few things."

"Anything in particular?"

"I made a wreck. I mean, I was in a wreck. And my wife."

She writes. "Was it a bad wreck?"

He remembers his call to the police on Saturday. Did he get his message to them? Do they know now that he's a killer? It would be just as well. He looks back to Mrs. Taylor. All these questions, leading up to the accident. Branscom and his threat of court. It all fits together. Whoever this is sitting before him is simply waiting for his confession. They can't fool him, though.

"How did the wreck happen?"

He shakes his head back and forth, knowingly. "I won't answer any more questions until I see my lawyer." He even smiles a little, pleased that he has figured out this plot before they had him.

"Do you think I want to hurt you in some way?"

He thinks of Jerry and Jean together. Where have they been meeting? In a motel? His house?

"Can we talk again tomorrow?" she asks as she stands up.

"I don't care," John says, already forgetting about the lawyer and the trap, the confusion swirling his thoughts together, making him dizzy.

"You try to rest for a while," she says as she leaves the room.

He gets up, closes the door to his room and lies down. When he wakes an hour later, his door is open. He wonders about this as he lies on the bed, still groggy, listening to the sounds coming from the halls and lounge.

Chapter 25

Why would she have to cry about it? It's what she wanted: asked him to stay home from work, said she was having what she thought were contractions, even though the baby is not due for another two weeks, asked him to hold her, and he did, wanting only to comfort her, not sure whether she was ready for the hospital or what. She's the one who started in with the huggy stuff, kissed him on the mouth and let her hand lay in his lap.

Frank puts the kettle on to make coffee and stands leaning against the yellowed linoleum counter top. He listens to her sobs as the water rumbles in the kettle. She's pretty, Frank thinks, not that he hasn't noticed before. Of course he has. It's just been a different sort of noticing he's done, knowing that her baby will be born without Luke, that she's going back home to her folks to live. Get on welfare probably. Have a little social security from the years Luke held regular jobs—a few years from the mines, couple more working on the roads or some such make-work, several more pumping gas. The rest of his work, the logging and dozer work at the scab strip mines, doesn't count since the owners paid in cash to avoid paying taxes and social security.

Take a little, give a lot: Mingo County and West Virginia. He shakes his head, thinking about it. It's all been such a rip-off from the start. But Frank knows that the mine companies could not have gotten control of ninety percent of the land without the greed of the people and their ignorance of how the industrial system works. Greed and ignorance, all any man or group of men need to sell their souls and those of the next ten generations. He thinks of the story his great-granddad used to tell before he died, about the time he ran the railroad detectives off his bottom land with his rifle. "Fellers had a paper said they was gonna take my bottom land along the river," he used to start out. "I says, 'Who's gonna take this land? Not you two fellers. Take more'n the likes of you.'"

" 'But this paper gives the railroad the right of way.' "

"Right of way," the old man would scoff. " 'Stick your right of way out in the river, you want to build a railroad. Don't need no railroad down here. Best corn in the county grows right here.' "

" 'But the company has the *right*.' "

" 'Well, you bring that company out here, and I'll tell it what it can do.' Two fellers stood there kicking around in the dirt for a while, went over and talked a little and then come back and started off again about the law sayin' there could be a railroad across my land. Finally told 'em I'd count to ten and they'd best be off. They stood there looking at each other till I hit three, countin' real slow, had the hammer back by then, and they took off on the wagon path along the river like two coons with a hound a-bitin' at their backsides. Fired one into a tree beside 'em, just to let 'em know they didn't need to come back."

Frank opens the package of rolls he bought the day before, breaks off a couple of sections, and takes a big bite. The old man never went any further with the story though. Ended up with a railroad on his bottom land all right, nothing he could do about it in the end. Ruined his farm. Ended up working for the railroad in Williamson, hating every day he went down to the yards, hating even more the weeks away from home when he was assigned to the crews building the sidings for the new mines. Hated it, but he was strong. And smart. Lived to be ninety-seven, didn't let them get the best of him. Had his God and his Jesus to turn to, and nobody or no thing could get past those two to upset the old goat.

Frank pictures the leftover cabin on the hillside; nobody been living in it for years, one of his uncles the last to use it. But Frank's old man, who bought a little farm and moved back home five years ago, still tends after the place, going out with his scythe in the summer, keeping the weeds from covering up the porch, hikes up there and stays overnight sometimes. No roads near the place, just the cinder path along the railroad.

Frank takes the steaming coffee and rolls into the living room and sits on the couch beside Elly. She won't look at him, though. Finally, after holding the coffee cup toward her for several moments, he says, "You want this or not?"

She sniffs and looks at him.

"Yeah, I'm a mean son-of-a-bitch."

She takes the cup and quickly sets it on the small crate Frank uses for a table. "Hot," she says.

Frank eats another roll and sits back with his coffee. "You done crying?"

She nods and concentrates on the coffee cup.

"No need you feeling guilty for something that comes natural."

"Luke and the baby…."

"Luke's gone, and nobody thought more of him than me."

"He always talked good about you."

Frank gets up and switches on the black and white portable TV. In a few moments Phil Donahue comes into focus, and then the picture shifts to a woman sitting by herself on the small stage. She is talking about how women must dress to be accepted in the business world. "Blue is a good color," she says. "Dark blue, that is, with a contrasting blouse and perhaps a scarf to blend it all together. Studies have shown that certain styles of dress are more conducive to creating an aura of authority."

Frank gets up and switches the channel selector. "That's good," Elly tells him when one of her morning soap operas comes on. Frank sits with her as she becomes absorbed in watching the latest tragedies of the Palmer family unfold. The doctor's son is involved with a strange girl in the small town and doesn't know that her father is a figure in the mafia, but the doctor's mother knows this and is debating with her husband's first wife whether or not she should tell her son. The factory worker with the good body is making it with the doctor's daughter from his first marriage, and the two of them don't know they are first cousins.

Frank gets up and goes out to his truck. Might as well go in to work late, better than losing a whole day's pay.

John has been in the hospital a week, and Mark has been to see him a couple of times. He introduced Mark to several other patients: the alcoholic who sits all day vowing he'll never take another drink, the poet who is married to a rich businessman and comes in the hospital once a year, and the preacher who sits in the lounge reading his Bible and saying prayers for everyone who sits down beside him.

John's initial belief that he would be on the psych ward for only a week or so gradually crumbled as he got used to the place and got to know the patients. They tell each other things they won't tell their doctors, share intimate details of their lives with each other. John feels comfortable here, and though he has tried many times to convince himself that he wants to get out and back to work, back to the real world, he has not been successful. This is a good hideout, a safe haven where he can get a shot to make him feel good or put him to sleep. He'll ride out the stay here, make the best of it.

Mark figures Jean will be going to school, since she seemed so excited about her classes the past several weeks. He drives around the huge parking lot at the campus until he finds her car and parks a couple of rows behind it. He listens to the radio as students come and go, watches them, thinks about his own aborted attempts at education, and wonders what motivates all these people to go to school. Young people, a nun, an old man with a long beard, more variety here in dumpy Cranston than on the Columbus campus.

He rereads the letter from Amy that came in Saturday's mail. A pleasant surprise for him. She'll be home next weekend, says in her letter she wants to see him, and he'll try to get off Saturday night early, take her out to dinner or something, have a good time. He feels especially good that she signed her letter "Love."

The lunch hour passes, and Jean has not yet been to her car, causing Mark to wonder if he has the right one spotted. It looks like hers. About one-thirty he walks up to the Mustang. It has a black interior like hers, but there is nothing inside the car to identify it for sure. He wishes he could remember the license number. But he knows from talking to Jerry that her last class is over at two o'clock. Mark waits by one of the buildings.

Finally the class hour is over, and he watches as the students file out. Jean sees Mark at the same moment he sees her—coming out of the building with Higby, laughing at something he has said. Then Mark sees Higby, and looks again quickly to make sure he is seeing right--the bearded dude at the restaurant. He looks back to Jean, trying to see something in her face that will tell him what is happening and why, but can find only surprise.

"Mark," she finally says. "What are you doing here?"

He doesn't answer, just stands there blocking the sidewalk. Higby stands behind Jean, his briefcase hanging at his side. "Dad's in the hospital," Mark manages to say. "He almost died. Thought you might like to know." He turns away.

"What happened?"

"What do you care?" he says and turns away again.

She follows. "Please tell me what happened."

He keeps walking. "A week ago Saturday he got real drunk and took an overdose of his nerve medicine."

Jean is half-running alongside to keep up. "Is he all right?"

"Yeah, he's over the worst. He almost died." Mark stops and looks at her, trying to see if the information means anything to her. "Who's your boyfriend?"

Jean stands shaking her head. "I didn't think he would do anything like that."

"He's in Cranston General in the psychiatric ward.

But I don't think you should see him until you talk to his doctor."

"How did you know about me and Hank?"

"Hank? That his name? I saw you with him at a restaurant one night. Did you have a good dinner?"

Jean looks down, biting nervously at her lower lip, and Mark walks away, leaving her by herself in the parking   lot.

Chapter 26

John snubs out his cigarette as the stainless steel cart holding the shock machine is pushed past the lounge by a doctor. John knows they'll be to his room in a minute, and he is lying on the bed when they come in. His psychiatrist asks him how he's feeling this morning, and John answers, "Good."

It took a few days for the doctor to talk John into the shock treatments, but he felt so depressed he finally consented. "The quickest way out of depression," the doc told him about the treatments. The anesthesiologist eases the needle into John's arm. He lies very still and can feel himself drifting out of consciousness. Then he is awake again. The way it always is. All you remember is the needle being put in your arm. Then you wake up by yourself, find yourself on the bed with the rails up, your forehead warm, face flushed from the current just run through the system. John gets up right away this morning. The doctors and nurses say stay in bed, but most of the patients—once they get used to the treatments—get up right away and return to the lounge to have a cup of coffee or another smoke before breakfast.

John opens the blinds of the window and looks out as the dim light seeps in. Snow! He sits down on his bed and watches the fine crystals hitting against the window. The ground is wet, not ready to allow itself to be covered over. John, fuzzyheaded from the treatment, thinks that he has lost track of time. Winter already. But he looks at his watch calendar and sees that it's only the middle of October. He has been here only two weeks, just as he thought. He thinks of Jean, and the thought disturbs something deep inside him. He wonders what she is doing, but the thoughts hurt him. And he wonders now, as he sits on the bed, how he could have said he loved her only two weeks before. He hates her more than anything now. How can he repay her, hurt her the way she hurt him? A divorce, he thinks. That would fix her wagon. Have papers served on her, see what she thinks of that.

When he has taken his shower and is sitting in the lounge smoking and having coffee, he has begun formulating his plan. When the doctor comes by later this morning, John will ask him for a pass for the afternoon. Get out for the day and see Gene Cowley, get the paperwork started, see how Jean likes that. He grows excited. He'll have to call Gene to make an appointment. Call Mark to see if he can pick him up here at the hospital. Can drive his car back here later today, leave it in the parking lot, as many of the patients are allowed after they have been here a couple of weeks. He is in a good mood when Doctor Williams gets around to see him. The appointment with the lawyer is set, and Mark is waiting for John to call back to see what time he will need a ride.

"Do you think you're ready to go out?" the doctor asks him.

"I feel good. And there's some things I want to take care of in Oakridge."

"You seem to have it planned out well enough," the doctor says after John has explained how he will get around and so on. "If you get along all right, maybe you'll want to start getting out more often."

John hadn't thought of that. Get out more often. All he wants to do is get out now, throw a few punches and duck back into the hospital. The place is more of a home just now than John has anywhere else. But maybe there will be more things he'll want to get out and do. Just maybe he's got this thing licked.

His mood has not changed by the time Mark picks him up at one o'clock, and Mark notices the change, this renewal in John, the sense of purpose and energy that his father always seemed to have. Mark stays at the house for a few minutes to make sure John is okay by himself. But as they talk, Mark sees that he need have no worry. When Mark is gone, John finishes sorting out the mail and writes the checks for the several bills that have arrived during his absence. He is ready to leave for the two-thirty appointment with his lawyer, when he finds the paper on which he scribbled Frank's address a couple of weeks before. Take care of that today, too. He hasn't thought much about the accident this week. The hospital has been good for him so far. He'll see Branscom one of these days and thank him for forcing him to go there for treatment. Settle things with Jean today, be done with her, have the bank write a check to Elly. He puts the savings passbook in his shirt pocket and is on his way. He glances at his Oldsmobile in the garage as he gets in. Good as new again—Mark took care of getting it to the dealership for repairs while he was in the hospital.

Outline finally done for most of the book. Higby is so demanding. Made her rewrite the chapter four times before he would let her start on the second. She is tired and feels like lying down, but forces herself on with her work. She's got to do this thing, write the book. If she can't make it on her own...she can't even let herself consider that. She always had John to lean on before, but she doesn't plan on that anymore, not the way they parted. She called his doctor after she saw Mark, and he made an appointment for her to come in and see him. Wouldn't let her see John yet. Asked her all sorts of questions about her and John: their sex life, social activities, friends, everything personal about her life. Asked about her and Jerry Shunk. She tried to explain, but the doctor could not understand why she had to lie to John about whom she was talking to. Practically called her a liar when she insisted there was nothing but friendship between her and Jerry.

Jean watches the cars pass. The snow has turned to rain, turning the streets a muddy brown. She looks around her second floor apartment. She could have done worse. This place will do until she gets things moving, until maybe she can move in with Higby. They get along so well she finds it hard to take him seriously when he tells her not to make any sort of emotional attachment to him, says she's just going to hurt herself if she does.

She gets up from the desk and gets a soda. So dreamy and tired today, can't focus her thoughts on the book. Needs some time away from it, maybe. She opens the refrigerator and checks the marinating flank steaks. Back in the living room, she turns on the color television she took from the house the day she went back to get the rest of her things. Game shows and soap operas. She slumps back on the spongy sofa and takes a sip of her drink as a contestant on *The Price Is Right* jumps up and down and squeals with excitement. By the time *The*

Edge of Night is on, she is asleep.

"But is divorce what you really want?" Cowley asks John.

"She deserted me. I figured I'd go ahead and file, at least be done with worrying about it. You're the one who's always said that if you're going to fight a legal battle, try to get the first punch in."

"But you and Jean? It's just hard to understand." Cowley looks at John but can see no emotion on his face. Stony, cold about the thing, not like the John Holz he has known for so many years at the country club. "Okay. I'll get it drawn up. You going for everything?"

"Yeah," John answers quickly. "She's the one brought it all on. I've got any type of grounds you're interested in. Adultery, for starters."

Cowley is surprised. "Can you prove it?"

"Certain evidence would prove it."

"Anything specific?"

"No. I guess not."

"Let's not use that unless we have to."

"Okay," John says and shrugs again. "You'll take care of it then?"

"Yes. Where is she now?"

"I don't even know," John admits slowly.

"I'll need her address."

"You can dig that up, can't you?" John is a little irritated at not knowing Jean's address. How can the sheriff serve the papers on her if they don't know where she lives?

"Do you have any idea where she might be?"

"Cranston. She's going to college there. They ought

to have her new address. If she's not there," he says, getting an idea, "just announce in the newspaper that a divorce has been filed and she's got so many days to make her presence known or the divorce will be final— you know, like you see in the paper once in a while."

"I'll try to find out her address."

In a few minutes John is walking through the cold, drizzling rain toward the bank. He is still excited, glad to be settling these troubling parts of his life. Get this stuff out of the way and get back in the groove. He feels powerful as he pulls open the heavy door at the bank. What was it he was going to pay her? Two thousand? Make it five. Give her an offer she can't refuse. Five grand, tax free. "May I help you?" asks the young woman at the teller's window.

"You certainly can. I want a bank check for five thousand dollars made out to Elly Baker." John writes the name on a form the teller gives him.

She takes the passbook and puts it in the computer to add the interest from the last quarter. Soon she has the check made out and the amount deducted from John's account.

"I'd like to have the check sent in one of the bank's envelopes," John tells her. She takes the address John gives her to a secretary and returns in a minute with an addressed envelope.

Back in his car, the check mailed, John decides to stop by the Metal Works. But when he is there a few minutes later he drives on past. Back home, he is beginning to feel tired. His hospital pass is good until five o'clock, but he decides to go back early. While he is packing clean clothes, he ponders the nearly empty side of the closet, which was not so long ago filled with

Jean's clothing. He feels confused as he snaps his suitcase together, and hurries outside. He stops as he is backing out the driveway and looks at the house, some thought deep inside trying to force its way to his conscious mind. But nothing comes, just the fatigue and anxiety suddenly come upon him. He hurries back to the hospital.

The feelings stick with him all evening. He tries to figure out what it is that's bugging him, but can get nowhere. Finally, at nine o'clock, he asks for one of the shots the doctor has on order for him.

He lies on his bed waiting for the thing to take effect. But after a half hour or so he can feel little difference, some thought still trying to nag its way into his conscious mind, and he goes out to the lounge to have a smoke. Tonight is bingo night, and a student nurse is busily handing out the cards and buttons to the patients who want to play. John sits and watches them. About ten o'clock he starts to feel drowsy and starts back for his room. "Bingo!" the preacher shouts as he goes through the doorway.

The phone in the hallway rings at twelve-thirty, and Mark dashes out of his room to answer it. Amy said she would call as soon as she got to town, and it is her. Mark is excited, and says he'll be out to pick her up right away. Talked one of the other guys at the station into trading him Saturday for Monday. Cost him five bucks, but it will be worth it.

"Give me an hour or so," she tells him.

"Okay. You want to go out to dinner tonight? Maybe catch a movie later?"

She considers. "I think Mom and Dad are expecting me to have dinner with them. Let's see how everything happens today. Okay?"

"Sure. See you in about an hour."

Finally her, finally get to see her again. He sits in his easy chair listening to the radio. He's restless, keeps looking at his watch, gets a beer and sips on it, looks through the copy of *Walden* that he kept when he sold the rest of his books at school. He sees where Thoreau listed the costs of building his cabin, and Mark envisions himself with Amy in some similar environment.

He pictures himself standing in his bean patch, wiping the sweat from his brow, and Amy is coming up the slope from the pond, leading a toddler by the hand. Her hair is long and brushed, the sunlight glinting gold off it. But where does the child fit in? Mark wonders. Thoreau never had any children to care for. If he had, Mark wonders if he would have been out in the woods instead of learning a trade in Concord, joining the rest of mankind in their plodding lives of quiet desperation. A disturbing thought at the very least, imagining Thoreau with eight or ten children to feed, house and clothe. Take a hell of a bean patch to feed ten people.

After waiting forty-five minutes, Mark is on his way to Blatt's house. The day is cold; the early chill never retreated enough for there to be much of an Indian summer, but today huge puffs of fleecy-white clouds sail overhead through sunshine. As Mark drives through the pine forest a few minutes later, he thinks again of Thoreau. So simple, this system of nature, propagating and killing in its valueless ways.

The park is mostly deserted this time of year, and as Mark parks behind Amy's Camaro he thinks he'll ask her to go for a walk.

Amy comes to the door, and as Mark steps into the foyer he leans to kiss her. "Hi," he calls to the Blatts as he follows Amy across the slate floor.

"How are you, Mark?" Bill says and stands up to shake hands.

"Real well," he says and looks to Millie.

"How's John getting along?"

"He seems to be doing well. Got out for a few hours the other day to run some errands."

"He'll be out pretty soon, then?"

"*Where* on earth has Jean been?" Millie interrupts. "I've tried to call her a dozen times at least, and she's never home. She even missed the luncheon at the club Wednesday."

Mark studies the pinned oak flooring which the Persian rug only partly covers. Then he sees the confused look on her face and explains the best he can. "She and Dad had a fight a couple weeks ago, and she left the house. She got an apartment somewhere in Cranston to let things blow over. I think she's waiting to come back home when Dad gets out of the hospital. They can sort of start over again together."

"That's terrible," Millie says.

Mark nods assent and looks at Amy. She sits quietly at the far end of the long couch. "Well," Bill says and gets up, "I've got to get over to the park office. The kids keep throwing their beer bottles and trash along the park road where our lane turns off, and I'm going to get something done about it."

"And I have got to get to the market," Millie says. "Will you join us for dinner tonight, Mark?"

He looks quickly to Amy. "Thank you. That would

be nice."

"Sounds like real problems for your parents," Amy says.

"I can't quite figure it out. It's a lot more complicated than I let on. I think Mom's seeing another man."

"You're kidding. *Jean*?"

Mark nods glumly. "But that's their problem. I can tell them what I think about the whole thing, but they're not telling me what to do anymore, so I can't really expect that they should listen to any advice I might give them."

Amy sits quietly. "Hey, it's nothing for you to be concerned about," he says. "They've got their lives and I've got mine. It's their problem." She nods agreement. He puts his arm around her shoulders, and she snuggles to him. She seems older, somehow, Mark is thinking. Quieter. "I've thought about you a lot," he says.

"Me too," she says. "A whole lot."

She seems happy when he suggests they take a walk. "Think we can make it clear around the lake?" she asks when they are outside.

"Sure. It's only a couple of miles. So how's school going?"

"Pretty good so far. Got all A's and B's on my midterms."

"That's really good."

"Have to keep my grades up. There's still too many teachers for the openings in special ed now."

"The odds aren't so good," Mark says. She nods. He puts his arm around her, reaches her waist on the other side, and pulls her close. They walk, occasionally scattering the leaves from the maples along the shore. Mostly it is a pine needle floor in the forest, and the air is sweet with the sap of the big trees. They reach the point where the land extends into the lake and watch two fishermen in a rowboat. "Nice weather for a change," he says to break the silence. They walk off the point, and Mark pulls her close and kisses her. She kisses him, but a little half-heartedly, it seems to him. He thinks maybe that he has made a mistake in feeling she might like him as much as he likes her. But he can't believe that so easily. "What's the matter?" he asks.

She shakes her head, not sure how to tell him her feelings.

"Is it me?" She shakes her head. Tears are rolling down her cheeks now, and he forces her face around to his. She looks into his eyes and seems reassured.

"We've got a problem," she says, wiping away the tears.

Mark doesn't understand. "You don't owe me anything. I mean, if it's another guy or something. It's not like we were going together or anything."

"I'm pregnant."

Mark frowns as the shock of it comes to him. She watches now as he lowers his head. "Me?" he finally says.

"I knew you'd say that!"

"But, I mean, it was only that one time. Don't you take the pill or anything?"

"I guess I've got my answer," she says and starts down the trail.

"Wait a minute," he shouts, and runs after her. He catches up and spins her around. "I didn't give you any answer. There wasn't even a question."

"You had to ask if it was your baby. What do you think?—I go to bed with a different guy every night?"

She is angry now, but so is he. "No, I don't think that."

"I should have just gone ahead and gotten the abortion. I wasn't even going to tell you, but I thought maybe." She shakes her head and starts off again.

"Abortion? My baby and you weren't even going to tell me?"

"Not so loud."

"Well, then quit running away." They stand watching the rowboat. "Okay, so we've got a problem," he says. "There's solutions." She nods. "We, you can have an abortion." She starts to say something, but nothing comes out. "Or you can have the baby, and we can get married."

"That's what I thought, too."

"I've never thought about being married to anybody."

"Me either."

"I'll marry you," he says.

She looks at him and laughs. "Were you going to ask me to marry you today?"

"No, I just wanted to see you."

"A baby shouldn't be the reason for a marriage."

"Maybe not, but we've got a lot more going than just the baby."

He feels strange saying the word. Baby. His baby and hers. "All our lives I've admired you. Let's get married."

"I don't know." She takes a couple steps toward the water. "I just don't want us to do anything that is going to determine the rest of our lives, unless you really want to."

"You don't know if you want to marry me?"

She nods. He's got to make a stronger showing than

this. He walks around in a circle.

She can't tell for sure. Does he really want her, love her enough for them to try to make a life together? Maybe in a couple weeks she'll know for sure whether he cares for her the way she knows she can grow to care for him. It would be so easy for her to say yes, and have the two of them rush off and get married. But if he's not ready…and there'll be the baby. She would rather have the abortion than have a child by a man she isn't sure wants her forever.

"I can get an abortion any time for the next month or so. We can wait to decide."

"How long?"

"Two weeks? I'll be back home then, and we'll decide for sure."

"All right. I'll marry you in two weeks." He takes her hand firmly in his and pulls her along to finish their walk around the lake.

"Slow down," she laughs after they have gone a short way. "We don't need to run."

"Yeah," he says, holding her hand tightly.

Chapter 27

Starting up a couple of old mines near Vulcan. Could probably get on at one of them. But what a way to live. Spend your life crawling around on your hands and knees, never get the feeling you're clean, the coal dust filling all the pores of your body. Good for the economy, though. Take people off welfare, get them going again. But it won't last; the economy or the companies will put an end to it, just about the time the area starts getting some health. The way it always happens. The way it's happened for ninety years. A one- industry culture is no good.

Frank gets up and paces the small room. He stops and looks to the parking lot below, sees by the mercury lamps his dull truck parked among the shining vehicles there, and looks at his watch. How much longer can this go on? Been here since noon. Ten hours already and no baby. In to see her several times till the nurse made him leave the room.

Frank the father. He wonders what Elly will think when she sees him listed as the father on the birth certificate. No other way to go about it, never thought before this morning that he would have to be listed as the father for his hospital insurance to work. Same last name, though. Hell, he just did what he had to do.

Wouldn't take much to get started in the cabin. Maybe the five hundred he has saved back would get them through the winter until he could find a job or start some kind of business, maybe join his uncle in his cabinet business. But Frank's cousin just got married and is working with him. Not really room for another this soon. The only way to be sure he could make it would be to get there in the spring, get the garden in early, put up enough vegetables for a year, make the jam and jelly, maybe buy a calf to butcher in the fall. Could hunt for the rest of their meat. Still plenty of deer, rabbits, squirrels. Could probably get on welfare, but the thought of it is depressing.

Frank knows he'll end up down home, knows it for sure now as he has grown close to Elly in the weeks she stayed with him, as they talked of returning to the old ways of the mountains, where neighbors are more than just the people who accidentally end up living beside you. Oh, there's the bums, for sure, but when you're in trouble, out of money, or your house or barn burns down, there'll be somebody find a way to help you along. That's *real* welfare, Frank thinks. Give you food, build a new barn for you, maybe fifteen or twenty men show up at dawn on a Saturday and set to work. And around eleven the women and younger children start arriving, bringing with them a potluck feast. Work and the dinner, and later a dance and some music.

Frank sits pondering his feelings. He thought he was here for good. If it weren't for Elly and the baby, he would still think he was in the right place, earning a boring but comfortable living here in Oakridge. But now. It's all changed so much in the last few weeks. Her asking him to hug her or hold her, burying her flushed cheek between his neck and shoulder, light on him, her big stomach held close against him.

Frank keeps picturing the cabin. He could live there, knows he'd find some way to make it. With Elly and the baby. He gets up and paces again, and as he turns away from the window glimpses a nurse hurrying toward the waiting room from the hallway connecting the several delivery rooms. Then she is in the room with him. "Baker," she says. Frank steps toward her, and she holds out a clipboard to him. "Sign where the X is marked," she tells him.

"What's the matter?"

"Your wife is having some problems. The doctor may have to perform a caesarian operation, but we need you to sign for it."

He scribbles his signature on the paper.

She turns around and hurries toward the door.

"Can I see her?"

The door closes behind her, and she faces him through the window, shaking her head no. "I hope it turns out okay," the other man tells Frank.

Frank looks at him and nods, then resumes his pacing. He knows how to pray, and now is the time. Frank never prays for himself. Real prayer is not for oneself. No one ever told him that; he just knows. In a few moments Frank sits up straight and proud. He has done all he can do. Frank waits calmly, relaxed now.

A slow night. Mark sits watching the infrequent cars. Nothing going on in Oakridge on Monday night. He looks back to the copy of *Walden*. Told Clint to go on home, he'd take care of things at the station. Felt sorry for him tonight. Guy gets up and teaches school all day, then pumps gas for another six hours. Had a cold and fever tonight, felt really bad. Mark thinks maybe it would be a good idea to tell Clint to take off early every few nights. Walt never stops by the station, wouldn't ever find out. "Don't call me unless the place is on fire or there's a robbery," he told Mark after he had been there for a week or so.

Mark is tolerating his job, but that's about it. He can't save much on his low wages, and he wonders how he's going to take care of Amy and their baby. He's been going around to factories, but winter is the slow season for most of them, and things are already bad, with hundreds laid off. He had one good lead—McDonald's advertised for a manager—but Mark didn't get the job. He's glad he didn't. Who wants to smell like a hamburger for the rest of his life? Something will turn up. Mark is sure of that. Everything will work out, he tells himself as he marks his book page and walks out to the pumps. He will handle it. He and Amy.

Saw John this morning. He seemed quieter than on Friday, seemed to have lost most of the energy he had then, but Mark thought he looked good.

Starting a part-time job in the morning, delivering flowers and fruit and gifts for a local business. Can pick up an extra thirty or forty bucks a week there. He'll make it somehow, he thinks as he shivers against the cold wind sweeping across the station lot. He wishes Amy were in town so they could make some definite plans. Look for a house, maybe; just talk, love. He does love her. And it's not just the baby. When he thinks of her, everything feels right and symmetrical, all his feelings in balance about Amy, her beauty and grace.

Mark expected Frank to laugh. But he had to share his news with somebody, and Frank was the only one he could trust or want to share this personal news with. Congratulations, Frank said, and shook Mark's hand. A serious Frank Baker. Mark never saw much of that side of Frank before. Asked him when the wedding was, and Mark had to tell him he didn't know for sure. Couldn't tell him that abortion was still officially an open option, as far as Amy was concerned. Just couldn't tell Frank that for some reason, couldn't share the whole thing even with Frank.

Come on down home and get married, Frank told him. Be taking Elly back in a week or so, after the baby is born. Running away to get married, aren't you? West Virginia's the best place. Even got a cousin who's a preacher. Marry you for nothing. Set you up in your own little paradise for a few days, up on the mountain, nothing there but you and Amy. Mark pictures what Frank described about the cabin on the mountain as he runs the credit card through the machine. Would be a cheap way to have a honeymoon, the only way really. He can't blow all his savings on a wedding trip, not with a child on the way.

"Thank you," Mark tells the customer as he hands the receipt through the window. He pulls his collar up as he walks to the station office. Getting colder. Feels good in a way to be out here every day in the elements. Feels cold, but good too. Back at the desk, he tries to get into the ant war, but it doesn't interest him. Winter. Then spring. And a baby. He doesn't even know the due date, and counts the months out mentally. About June first of next year he'll be a father. No, he's already a father. Became a father in a hayfield. Beats the hell out of the back seat of a car, he thinks, and wonders where he was conceived.

Higby chuckles to himself from his seat at the bar.

Got her half loaded tonight, with all the drinks he's bought her for the last couple of hours. Got her going, and old Hank will take care of her in a little while.

Higby orders another beer. Getting loaded. Past even caring about the hangover he'll have in the morning. Hasn't missed a day of classes this term. Sleep in, to hell with all stuff he has to put up with. Time for a day off.

Linda bounces onto the stool beside Higby and takes a sip of rum and coke. "Beautiful, baby. Beautiful." Higby clutches the vinyl trim along the edge of the bar as his sense of balance momentarily deserts him.

Frank is by himself in the waiting room when the nurse comes back to tell him he can see his wife and son. He hurries to catch up with her. Everything all right? Elly okay? The baby got everything he's supposed to have? She laughs, stopping before Elly's room. "Yes. Everything turned out fine. The caesarian wasn't necessary."

He sees Elly lying on the bed, an intravenous fluid bottle hung on the stainless steel rack. He leans closer to look at her. She is asleep, the anaesthetic hangover controlling her. Then the nurse is at the door again.

Frank looks up from his chair and sees a bundle of thick white blankets cradled in her arms. The nurse is smiling. "He looks like you," she says, and hands the bundle to Frank. Then he sees the little red face squinting up at him. He smiles, a huge grin spreading across his face, and looks back to the nurse. Thin blond hair covers the baby's head, and Frank carefully runs his calloused palm across the fuzzy crown. Pouchy red cheeks, white in the center. Like maybe he's cold, the healthy colors coming with the weather. The baby wakes and reaches for the mother's breast, seeking, but finding Frank's hard chest. Then the baby is squalling. Frank looks up to the nurse and holds his son toward her.

"He's just hungry."

He sits beside the bed until Elly wakes and glances around the room.

"I got to see him," Frank says. "A handsome and strong boy he is." He holds his arms out to show the length of the baby.

Elly relaxes and smiles. She hurts bad., but she doesn't let on. Her baby is all right. She reaches her hand to Frank, and he takes it and holds it, rambling on about how the baby looks like her and Luke, and well, a little like him, too, now that he stops to think about it. She feels good, lying there listening to him go on about her child. She thinks of Luke for a moment. His son and he's not here to see him. But she's sure he's looking on from somewhere, happy that the passage of birth was made. She grips Frank's hand harder, and he smiles in return, feeling strange in his role of father and husband-to-be.

Elly is feeling drowsy again and is dozing off when she opens her eyes. "This is going to cost a lot of money."

"No problem. My insurance will take care of it."

"But it will be a lot of money."

He nods. He hadn't really thought about that part of the plan. When the insurance company finds out what Frank has done with his medical card, the law might be after him. Well, let them try to find him. He's done what he thought he had to do. He kisses Elly's cheek as she dozes off.

At his apartment later, Frank sits at the kitchen table looking over the day's mail—a mailer from the local discount store and a letter from the National Bank of Oakridge. The advertisement he throws away, and then he starts to tear open the bank envelope. But it's to Elly; he has no business opening it. He puts the envelope in the top drawer of his dresser. Whatever it is, it can wait until Elly is out of the hospital.

Chapter 28

John sits up, gripping the steel bedrails tightly. Wakes up angry from his shock treatments now. Chased the orderly out of the room the last time. Could have strapped him down if they had wanted to, John realized. Probably would have, if he had hit him. But he just wanted him out of the room.

He pushes hard against the rails and feels them bend a little. Why should he sit here like this? Blank-minded from the treatment, letting whatever feelings out that want out. Tears and rage. His desire for a cigarette eventually overrules his anger, and he goes to the lounge. He inhales deeply, the phlegm hanging heavily in his throat. His mouth feels very dry. That way all the time now—the dry mouth, because of the Elavil.

He doesn't know how much more of this he can take. He's tired of sitting in the lounge here, has heard everybody's life stories enough times to write books about them. "It just gets lonely," the widow, his friend, always starts out. "I don't know what I'll do," the young black man says. "One day she just came home and said she was leaving. One of my best friends, even!" he'll say before launching into his story. "No more booze for me," the mousy-haired alcoholic says. An hour later he'll tell the story about the time he and a buddy stayed drunk from Ohio to California, laughing as he remembers the camaraderie and daring adventure he connects with the trip.

John's sick of it. He wants out. He's had eleven treatments so far. One more, on Friday, to have the twelve that Doctor Williams originally scheduled. He'll be free to go then. He started calling the bank every couple days and can't understand why the check hasn't been cashed yet. You just don't let five grand sit around.

Doctor Williams keeps asking John what he thinks about when he wakes up from the treatments. John shrugs. He really doesn't know. The anger just comes out. But a couple of days ago he did wake up with something in his head, though he couldn't tell the doctor. He flashed a picture of a car engine, a big, eight cylinder thing like he has in his Oldsmobile. He could hear the whining strength of the engine as it was accelerated, could hear it shifting gears, finally pictured the car it was pushing along at a hundred miles an hour. A lethal weapon. But then came his revelation: If the internal combustion engine had never been invented, if technology had not progressed to the point at which oil could be refined to fuel the engine, if Henry Ford had never pioneered the mass production of automobiles, if cars did not exist, then John Holz would not be a murderer. And as he sits in the lounge smoking, he thinks these thoughts again, but they make less sense than on Monday. Much, much less, but his thinking is not clear enough for him to pursue it.

"I'm leaving today," the widow announces to John.

"Great," he says. As bored as he's been lately, he is usually glad to talk to her. She hands him an envelope and gets up, wishing him good luck. He wishes her the same, and by the time he opens the envelope she is gone. He reads the note. "I've been lonely. You'll be lonely when you're divorced. Come see me anytime." He looks at her address; he knows that area of Cranston. Yeah, it might be nice. She's nice-looking, though not nearly as pretty as Jean.

Jean sits before the electric typewriter she bought. She is able to make faster progress on the book now, at least once she gets started into a chapter. It's hard, she thinks as she takes a momentary break and watches the traffic on the busy street. But she feels good when she makes some headway, however slight.

She continues:

The copper casket was surrounded by flowers, dozens of arrangements sent by family and friends. There was one from the local Grange, and another from the 4-H group she had helped with until her untimely death. Henry, feeling strange and displaced in the dark blue suit his daughter had picked out for him, approached the casket for the last time. He didn't want to look again, but he let his family propel him to the casket before it was closed for the last time. He saw Ruth's ashen face, strangely dry-looking with the makeup and powder she never wore when she....

The doorbell rings, and Jean gets up slowly, thinking that it must be Higby. They haven't been together much in the last week, both of them working hard. She opens the door to find a law officer standing there.

"Jean Holz?" he asks her.

"Yes," she says, thinking that surely something has happened to Mark or John and that he is here to convey the grisly information.

"I'm Deputy Smith from the county sheriff's department, and I have a suit here that has been filed against you." He hands her the manuscript comprising the divorce suit, and she wonders why anyone would want to sue her. Then she sees. She looks back at the officer. "Sign here, please," he tells her and extends a small notebook.

In a few minutes she is reading through the suit, which charges her with gross neglect of duty and extreme cruelty, along with desertion. John is asking for everything they own. She cannot believe that this has happened. A divorce? Well, yes, she was expecting something to happen to clarify her relationship with John, but this seems so sudden. He never even asked her if she wanted a divorce for sure. She didn't think that *he* did. A divorce is just so final. She looks at her typewriter, which sits purring quietly. She decides to go to Higby. She will have him. He will help.

By the time she reaches Higby's place, the divorce is amusing to her. Imagine, John cooking up this thing, filing a divorce action against her. And just like him to want all the financial accumulations of their twenty years together. John the money man, she scoffs to herself.

When Higby opens the door, Jean still has the amused expression on her face. She kisses Higby, breezes into the living room and sits down.

"You look like you're into a good thing today," he calls to her.

"Sort of," she says as he enters the living room. She pulls him to her and kisses him. In a few minutes, they are in the bedroom. Higby has never seen her this hungry, except maybe the first time they were in bed.

Afterwards they lie for several minutes, Jean resting her head on the curly hair of his chest, the musky, man scent filling her. Finally he rolls to the side, and they lie together. "Nice?" she asks him.

"Nice."

"Do you think we could be together more?"

Higby pulls away and leans on his elbow. "Aren't we together enough?"

"I mean something that means more, just be together more."

"Uh-oh. You're not getting around to that stuff about living together again, are you?"

"Sort of. Say I am. What would you think about it?"

"Wouldn't work," he says.

"Why not?"

He sits up and leans against the headboard. "We've been over this before. My job, your husband."

"He's filed for a divorce."

Higby shakes his head. "I've told you before that I can't make any sort of commitments. You have no right to ask them."

She sits up with him and takes him in her arms and kisses him, but he doesn't respond. "Hasn't it been good between us?"

"Sure. It's been good."

"Well?"

"Listen, let's not talk about this. There's no way I want to be committed to anything more than my writing."

"But you wouldn't have to give up that commitment. That's ridiculous. I write, too, you know."

Higby looks at her in frustration.

"But I love you," she tells him.

He gets up and puts on his robe.

"What's the matter?"

He shakes his head and goes into the other room. In a minute she is dressed and there beside him. "Can you say that you don't love me?"

"I never said that I *did* love you. Why should I say I don't?"

"You can't mean that. The things we've had together...."

Higby gets up. "No. I'm not getting saddled down in some stinking, little town like this. I'm moving on as soon as I can. I don't need any extra baggage."

She looks up to him in horror. How had she so badly misjudged?

Higby is standing by his desk now. The tears start as she hurries to the door.

Jean the fool, she thinks, squinting out the windshield through the veil of tears. But she had to try, had to reach out from the boredom her life had become. She knows she would do it all again. Jean the writer. Such a bitter joke her ambitions have played on her.

Back at her apartment, Jean sits. She cries at intervals as the thoughts that she has lost everything keep coming. But the tears subside as she thinks out the possibilities open to her—she can go to John, can get a job here in Cranston and continue writing, can fight back in a divorce suit of her own so that John cannot take everything. She wonders what John would think if she came to him. Just at the time they were securely beyond the restraints of economic worries, beyond the point at which they had to look out for Mark's best interests, things got all screwed up.

She can take care of herself. She can get a job

teaching school. It would still involve a radical change in what she has expected would happen, but the thought of it does not frighten her. She'll fight, and keep her freedom.

After she has made an appointment to see a lawyer the next morning, Jean sits on the old sofa for a long time. The television is on, but she can't follow any of the programs, just keeps wishing it were already tomorrow so she could take some action to straighten things out. Get things moving. At eight o'clock she takes a sleeping pill and lies on the lumpy mattress in the bedroom, waiting for the pill to put her under. She tries not to think about Higby, but when she does she hears this mocking, little voice telling her, I told you so. She's doing exactly what Higby predicted she would do when the divorce got rolling—looking out for her own material and economic interests. She is glad when the barbiturate begins to take effect, as her thoughts are erased.

Chapter 29

Mark downshifts to second as the delivery truck approaches the stop sign. It's still hard to believe what Frank told him last night when he stopped by the station. Going down home. Marrying Elly. Going to raise baby Luke as his son. Got it all planned out. Leaving in the afternoon as soon as he gets his paycheck.

Talked to Amy on the phone last night. Said she wouldn't be here until Saturday evening, and she invited him to the cocktail party her parents are having. Amy wouldn't talk about their marriage, said she couldn't because there were so many people around and she hasn't told anyone yet. Good enough. But she gave the same excuse a few days earlier when Mark tried to get her to finalize their plans. He can't blame her if she doesn't want to marry him. Surely she is pretty enough and intelligent enough to have her pick of men, maybe grab a doctor or lawyer along the way. But an abortion sounds so terrible and ugly to him. Mark parks before Frank's apartment and wonders if he has been making a fool of himself by sticking to his plans of marrying Amy. She hasn't said yes. How many times is a man supposed to propose marriage before he gives up? He's told her enough times, he is thinking as he walks up the rickety stairs to see Frank. Enough times. Maybe he should wait until *she* asks *him* to marry her. Men and women are equal. Let her make the next move.

"It's open," Frank calls when Mark knocks. Boxes are stacked on the kitchen floor and counter, and Frank is sitting on the couch watching Elly change the baby's diapers. Mark sits down beside Frank and looks at the tiny, clutching figure. So small and fragile. So much he'll have to learn if he is to be a good father after Amy bears their child.

"Kid's got it made," Frank says. "Just eats and sleeps."

"He does more than that," Elly says as she takes the diaper pin out of her mouth and neatly pins the cloth. "He can play already." She holds her thumbs out to Luke's hands, and he grabs them for all he's worth. She stretches her arms out, pulling her thumbs back until the pressure breaks his grip. Then he is seeking the hands again. "See," Elly says to make her point. She picks him up, retreats to the chair in the far corner of the room and starts feeding him. "What time do you plan to leave?" Mark asks.

"Couple hours probably. Most of the stuff's packed. All of it really, except for a couple pieces of furniture that are mine." Frank gets two beers from the refrigerator. They sit for a while, Frank talking about his and Elly's plans, about how he's going to get the cabin in shape, and that's where they'll live. His cousin, the preacher, has a gas station near Vulcan and has promised Frank a job. "He's got an offer to take over a church in Logan, but hasn't been able to sell the gas station," Frank tells him. "But I might just buy the place."

Elly glances at Frank. "Aren't you going to tell him?"

"Yeah." Frank takes a swallow from the brown bottle. "Strange the way things worked out. When Elly was in the hospital, a letter from an Oakridge bank came, and I stuck it in my dresser. But this morning, when I'm packing my clothes, I run across the letter. Well, it wasn't a letter. It was a check. Five grand."

"It's hard to believe," Elly says. "Now Luke can have the things he needs."

"That sounds like what I need right now. When I get married and all."

"Let me show you how to get to Vulcan in case you and Amy decide to come down," Frank says. "Get you married for nothing." Frank starts the map on a piece of paper he finds in the kitchen. "You ever hear of Vulcan?"

"No."

"There's a pretty good story to the place. Once, when the Tug River flooded, it washed out a bridge at Vulcan. See, the river has filled up with silt from the strip mines all along it, and when they get a heavy rain it floods real easy. Just about wiped out Williamson last time it flooded. Anyways, here's Vulcan without a bridge anymore. And to get to the Kentucky side the people had to drive fifteen miles till they got to another bridge. Well, the mayor kept writing letters to Rockefeller, the governor, to get something done about the bridge. But the state kept stalling on building it. Finally the mayor started writing letters to Congressmen and Senators, but they gave him the runaround too. Then he got the idea of applying for foreign aid from Russia.

Mark laughs. "Foreign aid?"

"Yeah, like we give to poor countries. So he writes a letter to Brezhnev just for the hell of it, and a few weeks go by, and he gets a call from a Soviet Ambassador in Washington."

"All this really happened?"

"Sounds unbelievable, but it happened. Anyway, this ambassador made plans to visit the mayor of Vulcan to see if the Russians could help build the bridge. Finally the dude shows up, took him a long time to get from the airport to Vulcan because the roads are so bad, and he had to get to a phone every hour to check in with the Soviet Embassy in Washington. So the mayor of Vulcan welcomes the Russian Ambassador to his house trailer and explains that he used to have a house until the river washed it away." Frank takes a drink of his beer, and Mark sits trying to picture the Russian in West Virginia. "Then they got down to the business about the bridge. The ambassador doesn't have the authority to say sure, we'll build it, but thinks it looks promising, and after his hourly phone call to Washington, they decide to go for a walk up the holler. Well, they get back there a little ways, no roads, houses, civilization in sight, and the Russian dude throws his arms up in the air and starts talking real fast in Russian. The mayor, he just waits till the guy gets over his excitement and can talk in English again. So the mayor finally asks him what all that was about. 'Nobody knows where I am,' the Russian tells him. 'They can't see me out here. I'm free.'"

Mark sits laughing along with Frank and Elly. "So what about the bridge?" Mark asks.

"The state of West Virginia decided real quick they'd build it. Must have been worried they'd end up with a bunch of Commie hillbillies or something. They sure didn't want to put Vulcan in the national news. How'd it look, people find out that one of the nation's former, top coal-producing regions is full of poor people the state won't even build a bridge for?"

"Really," Mark agrees and looks at his watch. "I have to make a couple more deliveries, and then I'll be done for the day," he says and finishes his beer. "You want to come along, I can help you load up later."

Frank looks at Elly, and she puts her finger to her mouth so they won't wake Luke. She tucks her breast back into the special bra Frank bought her.

"Yeah, sure. I'll come. I can't pick up my check until after one."

On the way out Frank gets the rest of the eight pack from the refrigerator. "Might get thirsty," he grins.

In the delivery truck Frank breaks out a couple beers. "Cheers," he says as Mark pulls away from the curb. Mark laughs and feels good as he raises the brown bottle. In a few minutes they are in the heart of Mark's delivery territory—out in suburbia where he grew up. He stops before a modest home and gets a flower arrangement from the back of the truck. Frank watches as Mark rings the bell and hands the flower basket to an old man. Maybe he should tell Mark where the five grand came from. But it doesn't matter, he tells himself.

At the edge of town Mark turns onto a long, asphalt driveway. They follow it for a couple tenths of a mile until the mansion is visible. "Who lives here?" Frank asks as he looks over the stately, brick home.

"Some doctor. Whitmore," Mark says as he looks at his delivery list. "He's a surgeon or something."

Mark gets a bushel basket out of the truck—oranges, apples, bananas, pineapples, all sorts of fresh fruit piled high in it, and struggles to carry it around to the back door. Frank gets out of the truck and walks into the garage. A huge blackboard in one corner catches his attention, and he walks over to check out the message on it. From the caretaker, something about the tractor needing a new power takeoff so the leaves can be mulched. Frank picks up a piece of chalk, grins, and prints neatly: THIRD WORLD, in big bold letters.

Frank is back on the driveway when Mark returns.

"Nobody home," Mark says and drops the basket along one wall of the garage. Frank finishes his beer and throws the bottle into the shrubbery.

John gets another cup of coffee from the pot in the lounge and sits by himself on one of the sofas. The doctor didn't make it around this morning, and John is glad he didn't. Here he is at the end of his treatment, still feeling like something is haywire.

A homely, young girl of about twenty sits down beside John and lights a cigarette, taking a huge drag from it and exhaling loudly. A new arrival. "This place gives me the creeps," she says through the cloud of smoke her violent sucking on the cigarette has caused.

"It grows on you."

She stares at him. "You give me the creeps, too."

John shakes his head and gets up.

She starts crying. "I didn't mean it. I don't know why I said it. I got fired from my job. I was a secretary," she calls after John.

He waits in his room for lunch to be served. Could get out tomorrow morning, Dr. Williams told him yesterday. If you feel like it. John doesn't know how he feels.

He wonders if the check has been cashed yet. He gets an outside line. "Miss Simpson, please."

"I was just thinking I should send you a letter," Miss Simpson tells him. "The check was cashed this morning."

"Thank you. Thank you very much." He did it. It's done. A tremendous surge of energy courses through him, and in five minutes he has his leather suitcase packed and is at the nurses' station demanding that they get Dr. Williams on the line immediately. While the ward clerk dials the number, John shifts from foot to foot, can't keep still.

"He's ready to leave right now," he hears the girl say into the receiver. "I'll tell him." She looks up at John. "The doctor's still in the hospital, and he'll be up to see you as soon as possible."

"How long did he say it would be?"

"I don't think it will be too long."

"I'll wait fifteen minutes," John says evenly. "I've got things to do. My time is valuable, too, you know." He winks at the girl, and she turns away in confusion to her paperwork.

"And to what may we attribute this big change?" Mrs. Taylor asks as she comes out of the drug bank.

"I'm ready to get out."

"Why don't we go back to your room and get started on the paperwork to get you out of here," she smiles and walks ahead of him. She sits down with her clipboard. "Are you sure you're ready to go home today?"

"I feel great," John says. "No problems."

She looks skeptical and writes something. "Do you think that your good feeling will stay with you all day?"

"It's a sure thing. Hey, I feel great. No problems."

Still perplexed, she says, "But just an hour ago you were sitting in the lounge looking so lifeless and worried."

John laughs. "That was before I decided that if I was going to leave and get my health back, I just had to find the courage to do it."

"You don't think about harming yourself?"

"Nah. Why would I do that?"

She sits smiling. "I have never seen a patient change so suddenly."

He taps his forehead with his index finger. "It had to happen up here. I'm ready to get out."

Back at the desk, John sits waiting impatiently for his doctor. The jobless secretary stops beside John and tells him her head hurts.

"It'll quit someday," he tells her, and she goes on her way, staggering from the medication she's taken.

In an hour John has been discharged and is back in Oakridge. At home he wanders around the empty rooms, then looks through the mail. A fancy, white envelope catches his attention. When he opens it, he finds an invitation to the Blatts' cocktail party the next night. Sure, he'll go to that—be fun getting back into things. Then he remembers the widow. Might as well get things off to a good start, he thinks, picturing her well-preserved figure and pleasant face as he dials her number.

The date set with her for the next night, John sits down in the living room and tries to read a newspaper. But he can't concentrate on it. He walks around the house, beginning to feel the emptiness of the place. There's always been someone else here with him—Jean or Mark—and he realizes that he's going to have to find something to do.

In a few minutes he is wearing one of his business suits and is on his way to the metal works. Get back into things right away, get back to normal. Work he knows how to do, he tells himself a few minutes later as he parks in front of the factory.

Jean opens her car door in the Cranston Board of Education parking lot. At least she's got a job now, though she doesn't yet know how much work she'll be offered as a substitute teacher. But there's a full-time job opening up in January, when one of the eighth grade English teachers is scheduled to go on maternity leave. The superintendent didn't promise it to her for sure, but she is confident that she made a good impression. And besides, she's a bargain— a mature teacher at the bottom of the pay scale.

But she'll supplement whatever she makes teaching with what John has to pay her. Her newly hired lawyer, after hearing her story, assured her that she would receive at least half of everything. "No way he can get everything," he told her, and said he would draw up a suit similar to the one John filed, asking for everything but John's underwear. She had to laugh at that. She'd like to see him with nothing more than his underwear. But she gets no pleasure from these thoughts. She is finding it hard to sustain her feelings of hate for John. So much has gone wrong and out of control. So much happened that she is ashamed and embarrassed for. But it seemed so real and natural for it to happen. The whole thing with Higby. And her writing. She can be good at it some day. She is sure of that. But why should it have estranged her from John? And how did she get involved with Higby? she asks herself. She *never* went out on John before. She's had her offers along the way, but never took anyone up on them. She is at a loss to explain her behavior. She doesn't understand it, and when she is back at her apartment she wonders what John would say if she went to see him. She decides to call him instead, and rings the hospital. "He was discharged this morning," comes the operator's answer when she asks for his room. She dials the home number in Oakridge. Maybe he will talk to her. She lets it ring a long time, and then sits on the couch, wondering if he is all right.

The apartment is drafty, and she thinks of the fireplace at home. How pleasant it was to have the fire going when it was cold. So many good times with John. And Mark, when they were a family. Sitting at her desk, she reads over the chapter she was working on yesterday. And she resumes the story where she left off, gets lost in making the typewriter follow her wishes, watching in fascination as she creates something which did not exist before she sat down at the desk.

John works until six o'clock, left by himself at five by the rest of the office crew. He's got to do it sometime, and he may as well get started off right. When he has gone over all the transactions of his best accounts, he is satisfied that he has put in a day's work today, even though he's been here only a few hours. On his way out, he startles the janitor, who is busily sweeping out the lobby while singing his own rendition of "Oh, Susannah."

It is dark when he gets home, and the solitude and silence are more imposing than earlier in the day. John looks through the cupboards for something to eat and settles on a can of baked beans. While he is standing beside the stove watching them bubble, he wonders what Jean is doing. As he sits eating, he thinks that if she were here he would be eating a beef roast or, at worst, maybe chili soup and crackers. She makes a good batch of chili.

He sits at the table after he has washed the leftover red slime from the plate, and wonders what he'll do now. In the hospital he didn't have to worry about what to do. If he wanted to smoke or talk, he'd go to the lounge. If he wanted to relax, he'd go and ask for one of his shots. But he doesn't even have any dope anymore. Doctor Williams didn't give him a prescription for anything except the Elavil, and he didn't think to ask for anything. On an impulse, he calls information in Cranston and gets Jean's number. But after he dials it, he wonders what he'll say to her, and at the third ring hangs up.

He's got to do something. He thinks of the maple in the back yard that he had planned to cut up for firewood. He takes his suit off and hurriedly puts on work clothes. At the patio door he stops and looks out into the dark yard. He flicks the switch, and the yard is awash with artificial light. Soon he has his chain saw buzzing away. He works on the smaller limbs for an hour. Then he attacks the main trunk. The chain saw drones on, and he finds that he can nearly stall the thing out if he puts a lot of pressure on it. He is on the second section of trunk when he hears a whistle behind him. He hits the kill button and turns around to find his neighbor standing there.

"What the hell you doing?"

"Cutting firewood."

"I can see that. It's almost ten o'clock, and you're out here with that thing."

"Oh," John says, not sure he likes the tone he's hearing. But company is company. He sets the chain saw down. "Get you a drink, Harry?" he asks.

"Not tonight, John," he says, moderating his tone now. "Got company," he says and turns away.

"Sorry about the noise," John calls after him. He stands beside the tree and the pile of wood for a while, tips one of the big trunk sections to its flat side, and goes after   his   wedges   and   sledge   hammer.

Chapter 30

After work Saturday evening, Mark relaxes before he showers. All day he's anticipated his meeting with Amy, wishing it was here sooner, but now that the time has come he forces himself to slow down. He still hasn't decided how to approach her, doesn't know for sure if he should get on his knees and beg her to marry him, or play it cool and let her make the move to determine the outcome.

After his shower, though, he shapes at least part of his evening. He looks in his closet at the blue blazer he had planned to wear to the cocktail party, and decides instead to wear a pair of jeans and a flannel shirt. He feels comfortable in the soft clothing and sits listening to his stereo while he has a beer. Around nine o'clock he decides it is time.

Dozens of cars crowd close to the Blatt mansion, and Mark wonders if he'll even have a chance to talk seriously to Amy with all these people here. He finds himself in the foyer by himself, the revels of the partiers coming to him from the living room and the family room.

He hooks his thumbs in his jean pockets and stands rocking on his heels, looking into the room full of people. They're all here again, he is thinking as he walks slowly toward the bar at the end of the family room. The Blatts, the Trumbulls, Shunks, Hillmans, Wilsons, Coopers, dozens of them been getting together like this for years.

"Hello, Mark," Jerry Shunk calls across the room and comes after him. He offers his hand, and Mark takes it and squeezes hard. "How are you?"

"Can't complain. Nobody'd listen if I did."

"There you go," Jerry says, and in a moment turns to go back to his little group.

Mark is surprised when he sees John coming from the bar with an attractive woman. She hangs on his arm, and Mark can't help noticing the diamond jewelry she is wearing, so much with the huge stones making up the necklace that it appears gaudy. She is wearing more makeup than he ever saw his mother wear. Then John sees him approaching, and a huge, energetic grin spreads across his face. He slaps Mark on the back, and introduces the widow to him.

"When did you get out?" Mark asks John.

"Yesterday. I was going to call you, but I got busy and forgot about it."

"Feeling good?"

"Real well," John says. "Everything just started to fit together all of a sudden." Elizabeth entwines her arm in his and looks up to him. She knows all about that sort of thing.

"I think I'll wander around," Mark says as John and the widow move to the couch with their drinks.

Mark finds Amy and Jean at the same time. They and Gertrude Shunk are standing together near the fireplace. He gets a beer from the catering service's bartender and walks toward them. Amy sees him first, and as she looks at him he meets her eyes, trying to see some hint as to how they will settle things for themselves and their baby. He kisses Jean first and then Amy. "What about me?" Gertrude asks, indignantly, and Mark smiles as he plants one on her cheek.

"I didn't know I was in such great demand."

"You look like you know you are," Gertrude says.

"How are you, Mom?"

"I'm okay. How are you? Still like your job and everything?"

He shrugs. "Only because it pays the rent and feeds me."

"I've got a new job too."

"Have you seen Dad?"

"Yes."

"Have you talked to him or anything?"

"I haven't had the chance. He appears to be occupied."

Mark nods, wants to tell her to go see him, sit down beside him and the widow, and let him compare, but he says nothing. "Hello, Mark," a voice booms from behind him. He turns and shakes hands with Bill Blatt. "Hi, Mr. Blatt." Father-in-law? Grandpa?

"How you been? Saw you pumping gas the other day." Mark nods. "Stop out at the plant one of these days. If you're going to be sticking around Oakridge, you might as well get a good job." Bill is a little tipsy, and winks at Amy as he turns away. Maybe she has told him, Mark thinks as he sees the silent exchange.

"I've been watching for you," Amy says as Gertrude and Jean turn to watch Henry Trumbull corral Gary Cooper's wife beside the bar. Sally is smiling, but looking furtively around the room as if she can't think of a polite way to get out of the situation. She doesn't know Henry well enough to tell him to go to hell. Gertrude raises her fist and punches the air, and Sally sees and raises her fist. Henry backs off, laughing, muttering about women. "Can we talk?" Amy asks when Mark turns back to her.

"Sure." She takes his arm and leads him to the library. Then they are seated on the leather couch. "You look nice tonight," he says. She is beautiful, he wants to tell her.

"Thank you. You look good, too." She kisses him, and they settle back into the massive sofa.

"Marry me," he says quietly. "I love you."

She hugs him tightly. She would rather have killed herself than their baby.

Jean finally sees her chance when the widow leaves John's side. As she approaches, he still has his back to her, and rather than speak, she touches his shoulder lightly. He turns to face her. "I tried to call you yesterday," she says, looking into his handsome and unworried face. He walks over to stand before the fireplace, and she follows. "We're still married, you know."

He watches the yellow and red flames shoot up the chimney. "By law," he says and looks quickly to her as these unplanned and unwanted words spill out.

She stays there with him, though. "Are you okay now?" she asks him, the concern evident in her voice.

"Yes." He looks to her, and their eyes meet. She had to know that.

"Good." They stand in silence, and John is trying to formulate something positive out of the deep hurt he feels when he thinks again of the accident. Still a murderer. No amount of hospitals or medicine will erase that. He takes a big slug of his drink.

"How did all this happen?" Jean asks.

"All what?"

She shrugs. "This." She gestures to the room and people around her. "Us. You. Me."

He gazes into the fire, trying to wipe away the thoughts of the accident and hospital which momentarily were there. "I think it is just...." But he can't continue and turns to her, a confused look on his face. He has to turn away when he meets her serious, seeking gaze. "I think," he says again, but there is nothing he can offer by way of explanation. Nothing he possesses—values, beliefs or rationalizations—can be formulated into words to explain how he and she came to be where they are at this moment. There is no foundation for him to base his answer upon, nothing solid there to rely on.

Then the widow is there with them again, and John introduces her to his wife. They are sickeningly pleasant to each other as John practices a mental exercise his doctor taught him. But it doesn't work, and he sees a crumpled, green car.

William Trent Pancoast
1949—

"Blue collar writer" is how the *Wall Street Journal* referred to William Trent Pancoast in 1986. By that time, his working-class-flavored short stories and essays had appeared in many Midwestern and international magazines and newspapers. Pancoast spent the next twenty years as the editor of a monthly union newspaper—the *Union Forum*—and as a die maker, while continuing to publish his fiction, essays, and editorials in the *Union Forum, Solidarity* magazine, *US News and World Report*, and numerous literary magazines.

The term "blue collar writer" suits Pancoast just fine. As he told the *WSJ*, "The reason I write about work is that that's just about damn near all I've ever done." In addition to his jobs of die maker, machinist, railroad section hand and brakeman, and construction laborer, Pancoast has been a high school English teacher and adjunct professor of English. The author supplements his blue collar writing credentials with a B.A. in English from the Ohio State University.

Pancoast is retired from the auto industry after thirty years as a die maker and union newspaper editor and lives in Ontario, Ohio.